Dawn's Big Move

**Other books by
Ann M. Martin**

Rachel Parker, Kindergarten Show-off
Eleven Kids, One Summer
Ma and Pa Dracula
Yours Turly, Shirley
Ten Kids, No Pets
Slam Book
Just a Summer Romance
Missing Since Monday
With You and Without You
Me and Katie (the Pest)
Stage Fright
Inside Out
Bummer Summer

BABY-SITTERS LITTLE SISTER series
THE BABY-SITTERS CLUB mysteries
THE BABY-SITTERS CLUB series
(see back of the book for a more complete listing)

Dawn's Big Move
Ann M. Martin

AN
APPLE
PAPERBACK

SCHOLASTIC INC.
New York Toronto London Auckland Sydney

Cover art by Hodges Soileau

If you purchased this book without a cover, you should be aware that this book is stolen property. It was reported as "unsold and destroyed" to the publisher, and neither the author nor the publisher has received any payment for this "stripped book."

No part of this publication may be reproduced in whole or in part, or stored in a retrieval system, or transmitted in any form or by any means, electronic, mechanical, photocopying, recording, or otherwise, without written permission of the publisher. For information regarding permission, write to Scholastic Inc., 730 Broadway, New York, NY 10003.

ISBN 0-590-47005-1

Copyright © 1993 by Ann M. Martin. All rights reserved. Published by Scholastic Inc. APPLE PAPERBACKS ® and THE BABY-SITTERS CLUB ® are registered trademarks of Scholastic Inc.

12 11 10 9 8 7 6 5 4 3 2 1   3 4 5 6 7 8/9

Printed in the U.S.A.   40

First Scholastic printing, September 1993

The author gratefully acknowledges
Peter Lerangis
for his help in
preparing this manuscript.

CHAPTER 1

"You add *what*?" asked my stepsister, Mary Anne. She looked up from the steaming wok on the kitchen stove.

"Arrowroot," I answered. "And keep stirring."

"*Arrowroot?*" Mary Anne said. "That sounds sickening."

"It's for thickening," I replied. Then I realized what I'd said. So I added, "Underthtand?"

We both started giggling. It was one of those days.

I don't know about you, but I go crazy in the early fall. Especially when the air is so cool and clear you can almost drink it. I just want to run around in the falling leaves and scream and sing. So what was I doing? Slaving in the kitchen with Mary Anne Spier, trying to make "Tofu Garden Delight."

Bet you're dying to know what that is. Well,

I wasn't too sure myself. But it's the name of this *excellent* stir-fry dish at a restaurant called The Source in Anaheim, California (that's close to where I'm from). Since Mary Anne and I had agreed to make dinner that night, I was determined to figure out the recipe. Even if it meant being cooped up on an incredible day.

You know what Mary Anne thinks? She's convinced I like the fall because in California the weather is the same all year round and there is no fall. Well, I *love* Mary Anne — she is my best friend in the world and I mean the *world* — but here's the news for all you East Coast dudes: *WRO-ONG*. There *are* seasons in California, and leaves *do* fall from trees. Okay, it's not as *vivid* as here, or as *cold*, but it has its own good points.

Here, by the way, is Stoneybrook, Connecticut. And I, by the way, am Dawn Schafer. My mom and I moved here from California when I was in seventh grade (I'm in eighth now). See, Mom grew up here and her parents still live here, so she figured she'd move back here after she and my dad divorced.

Yes, it's true. My parents live on opposite sides of the country, like bookends. Sometimes I tell people I have a "bicoastal family" because it sounds pretty cool. But let me tell you, it *feels* pretty awful.

You know what else? My brother, Jeff, lives

in California with my dad. He did move here originally with Mom and me, but he wasn't happy at all. He started having trouble in school and being really moody, and we finally realized he was homesick for Dad (and California). So after a lot of arguing and crying, my parents decided to let him live with Dad. I really, really, *really* miss him. He's ten years old, and I don't know, I feel weird not being around to see him grow up. I've been thinking about visiting Dad and Jeff again a *lot* lately.

I have been out there a few times. It's fun, but boy, is it hard to say good-bye. Plus my dad has this girlfriend named Carol, which makes things complicated. At first I didn't care for Carol. Okay, the truth — *I couldn't stand her*. She was always trying to act super-young, as if she could be my age, but she's like *thirty-two* or so. Actually, I don't mind her now. She acted her age once, and I was pretty impressed. I mean it, too. It happened when the whole Baby-sitters Club went out there to visit. (The BSC is a club I belong to. I'll tell you about it later.) One of our members, Stacey McGill, got a crush on some guy and started hanging around with him and his friends. Well, they were pretty wild — wild enough to wind up having a car accident. Nobody was hurt, thank goodness. But when Carol found out, instead of keeping it a secret (to be cool and get on our good side), she told my dad. I know it may sound weird, but I respected her after that. She was acting like a responsible grown-up.

Dad's thinking of marrying Carol, and that's another reason I want to go out there so badly. I mean, if she's going to be his wife (my *stepmother*) I should get to know her a little, right?

Anyway, that's the western side of my family. As for me and my mom, well, we haven't exactly let the grass grow under our feet. (Don't you love that expression? It means that we haven't just sat around doing nothing.) First of all, I joined the Baby-sitters Club. Because of that, I made eight fantastic friends, including Mary Anne Spier. And Mom has gotten involved with all kinds of local organizations. She also got involved with a *guy*! Who? Well, he was her high school sweetheart and his name is Richard Spier.

Yes, the father of Mary Anne, who, as you know, became my stepsister! You see, Mary Anne's mom died when she was a baby. Mary Anne doesn't even remember her, and Richard didn't talk about her at all for years. Her death left him shocked and heartbroken, and he could barely make it through the day. He even left Mary Anne with her grandparents for a long time, until he could pull himself together.

Eventually he took her back and raised her by himself. Now, he is not exactly Mr. Laid Back. With Mary Anne, he became incredibly strict. He made her wear little-girl clothes, keep her hair in pigtails, and come in for super-early curfews until *seventh grade*. Mary Anne hated that, but she forgives him. She says he was just worried about being a perfect mother *and* father.

Whatever.

Fortunately, he treats her like a true thirteen-year-old now. He's still kind of stuffy, and super-organized. (Make that mega-organized. *Turbo*-organized. I mean, he wears his shirts in a strict order each day so they wear out evenly.) But my mom liberated him. Now, how would you picture a woman who'd fall in love with Richard Spier? Guess again. My mom couldn't be more different. She's . . . well, easy-going, fun-loving, carefree, absentminded. . . .

Okay, okay, she's sort of a space cadet. Not always, but she does do some pretty strange things. In our house, it is not unusual to find a mitten in the refrigerator or a set of keys in the microwave. And it's kind of amazing we manage to eat regular dinners. Once I discovered raisins in my clam chowder. Another time she made a yogurt-based salad dressing with oregano and ground pepper — but we had to dump it because she used vanilla-flavored yogurt.

Ta-da. We are now on one of my favorite topics. Food. I am very careful about what I put in my body. I eat no red meat, and I find sugary things absolutely disgusting. Whole grains, sprouts, tofu, organic vegetables — I love natural, healthy foods.

Okay. Are you done saying "Ew" and pretending to barf? Good. A lot of kids feel the same way, but you know what? I'm shrugging. It doesn't matter to me. That's the way I am, and I'm pretty happy about it.

"Here it is!" I exclaimed, pulling from the cupboard a jar of arrowroot. (It's a white powder that looks a little like baking soda.)

"What does it taste like?" Mary Anne asked. "Wood?"

"No, Mary Anne," I replied patiently. "I mean, not that I *know* what wood tastes like. Arrowroot's like cornstarch, but not as gloppy. Now *keep stirring*! Look, the *bok choy*'s burning."

"The who?"

My stepsister, you may notice, is not a health food freak. But I love her anyway. Of all the people I've ever met, she is the most caring and sensitive. She can practically read my mind when I'm feeling terrible, and she is

6

the *best* listener. I am soooo lucky to have Mary Anne as a sister. The only thing I don't like doing with her is going to movies. She cries a lot in general, but at movies it's pretty embarrassing. I mean, when we saw *Pocketful of Miracles* at an oldies festival once, they practically had to call a flood warning.

I should also tell you that Mary Anne is the *only* BSC member with a steady boyfriend. His name is Logan Bruno and his looks are *número uno*. We are talking hunk. He has curly hair, blue eyes, a Southern accent, and he plays sports and likes to baby-sit.

No, he's not perfect. He can be bossy (Mary Anne broke up with him over that once) and he takes it way too personally when his sports friends tease him about his sitting. But other than that, he's pretty cool.

Now. Back to the drama of the stir-fried dinner. Act One, the Preparation. I threw in some vinegar and soy sauce and it began to smell delicious. Even Mary Anne agreed. I checked the rice on the back burner, and it was perfect.

Mary Anne dressed the salad we'd made (with a homemade, *plain*-yogurt-based dressing), and we were ready for . . .

Act Two. It began with the ringing of the doorbell and the opening of the front door. "What smells so *fabulous*?"

Enter my mom, Sharon Porter Schafer Spier. Wearing a summery-print oversized blouse and matching shorts, she breezed into the kitchen and gave her daughter and stepdaughter a kiss. "What a treat to come home to dinner!" she exclaimed.

She exited.

A few minutes later Richard Spier arrived, and he immediately set the table. (Forks and knives for him and Mary Anne, chopsticks for Mom and me.)

Act Three. Dinner.

Theme: Health food can taste good.

"My compliments to the chefs," Richard said.

"What's your secret?" Mom asked.

"The different textures," I explained.

"And the right amount of arrowroot," Mary Anne added.

Richard stopped chewing. "What?"

Mary Anne gave me a look. We both started laughing.

"Just eat, dear," Mom said with a smile.

Richard shrugged and munched. Before long we were all jabbering away. Well, not all. Richard doesn't jabber. He *speaks*, slowly and clearly. But even he was pretty psyched about something. You could see it in his eyes. It was the look he gets when he has something to say about the stock market (zzzzzz). But this time it was actually about something interesting.

"I was reading in the Stamford paper about the joint fund-raising event by the Chambers of Commerce of Stoneybrook and Lawrence-ville," he said. (Hang in there, it gets better.) "This, um, 'Run for Your Money,' I believe it's called? It looks interesting. Anyone can form a team — coworkers, families, friends — and there are all kinds of crazy events. You pay a fee to enter and the proceeds go to char-ities. I think Stoneybrook's donating to an or-ganization for the homeless, and Lawrence-ville chose a literacy program."

"I wonder if Kristy knows about this?" Mary Anne wondered.

"She's probably already assigned us to teams," I said.

"Wouldn't it be fun to get some of the little kids involved?" Mary Anne asked.

"Well, I was thinking that the four of *us* should enter something," Richard suggested.

Mom raised her eyebrows in surprise. (Rich-ard is not exactly athletic.)

Neither is Mary Anne. "I don't know, Dad," she said.

Richard stood up and pulled the newspaper out of his briefcase, which was lying by the wall. "Look, most of the events are not true sports competitions. For instance, potato sack races — "

" 'Midway games,' " Mom began reading, " 'tug-of-war, pie-eating contests, underwear race — ' "

"Underwear race?" Mary Anne said, blushing. (Yes, *blushing*.)

"That's the one we should enter!" I piped up.

Now it was Richard's turn to raise an eyebrow. "Yes, well, I'll take that under advisement."

(That's Richard's idea of humor.)

"I think it would be fun to enter as a family!" Mom said.

"Yeah, it would," Mary Anne replied.

I nodded. I know I should have been more excited, but when Mom said "as a family" I thought of Jeff and Dad. They would *love* to be in Run for Your Money. They're both athletic, and they have a great sense of humor.

And I realized again I was *dying* to see them.

"Dawn?" Mary Anne said. "Is something wrong?"

"Uh-uh," I answered. "I was just . . . thinking. You know, about Jeff and Dad." Then I made myself smile and chopsticked some dinner into my mouth.

10

Mom looked at me sympathetically. "Why don't you call them tonight?"

"Yeah, I guess I will," I said. I chewed on some *bok choy* for a minute. "Mom? Would it be, like, too expensive for me to go out and visit?"

Mom looked at Richard, who shrugged. "Well, we can book some tickets for Thanksgiving," Mom said.

"Okay," I replied. "That would be great, I guess."

I tried to sound happy, but I know I didn't. Thanksgiving was *months* away.

"Unfortunately, it's the closest school holiday," Richard added.

"I know . . ." I mumbled.

"You really miss them, don't you?" Mary Anne said.

My eyes started to well up. *My* eyes. The ones belonging to me, Dawn Schafer, who teases Mary Anne about being a water faucet at movies. Boy, was I bummed.

"I know how you feel," Mom said. "Look, Thanksgiving's not that far away. But I guess we *could* try to arrange a long weekend before then, if you're desperate to see them."

"No," I said, "that's okay. I can hold out."

I dug into my Tofu Garden Delight. I had this great need to stuff my mouth. If I didn't, I might blurt out that I was lying.

I did call home that night. Jeff answered the phone.

"Hi," I said. "It's your sister."

"Duh."

I ignored the snide remark. "How's it going?"

"Fine."

"Is school okay?"

"Yecch."

"Too bad."

"Guess what? In gym I won the home run derby. And guess what else? I came in fifth in the physical fitness contest, but that was out of a hundred and three kids. And I got an O on my book report. That's for Outstanding. It's like an A in the older grades. Or better."

Typical Jeff. He'll tell you everything eventually, but he won't answer a direct question.

"That's fantastic! And how's Dad?"

"Good."

I took a breath. "And Carol?"

"What about her?"

"Well . . . is Dad still going out with her?"

"Yeah."

He didn't sound too thrilled. "Jeff, are you being nice to her?"

"*Yes,*" he said, in a way that meant *no.*

I just had to ask the next question. "Has Dad said anything about marrying her yet?"

"Nope. You want to talk to him? He's right here."

"Sure."

After a moment Dad got on the phone. "Hi, Sunshine!"

"Hi, Dad. I miss you."

"I miss you, too. We just got back from roller skating at the beach. Jeff's getting too fast for me."

"Oh, I wish I could come out and see you!"

"Well, Thanksgiving's around the corner."

Yeah, a *far* corner, I thought. "Uh-huh."

We talked a little more. Carol was there, so she got on the phone for awhile.

After the conversation was over, I went to my room and looked out the window. The leaves on the old maple were starting to turn yellow.

I narrowed my eyes and tried to imagine it was a palm tree.

CHAPTER 2

*R*RRRRINNGG!

Horrors. It was 5:28 on a Friday afternoon. Starting time for our Baby-sitters Club meeting was still two minutes away, yet the phone was ringing already.

"Boy, are we popular," Claudia Kishi said. She picked up the receiver. "Hello, Baby-sitters Club. . . . Oh, hi, Mrs. Papadakis. . . . A week from Saturday at eleven? Um, let me find out."

She looked at Mary Anne, who was checking the record book. "Jessi, Kristy, and Stacey are free," Mary Anne said.

"I can't," Jessi Ramsey informed her. "I'm going away."

"I'll do it," Kristy volunteered. (Which made sense, because Kristy lives across the street from the Papadakises.)

"Kristy'll be there," Claudia said into the phone. "Great. Okay, 'bye."

There. You have just seen the BSC at work. Simple, huh? Parents call us, we set up sitting jobs. There are seven regular members (and two associates), so someone's always available. Well, almost always.

Our headquarters is Claudia's bedroom, because she's the only one of us who has her own phone with her own number. (Claud is the club vice-president.) We meet on Mondays, Wednesdays, and Fridays, from five-thirty to six. Most of our business comes from regular clients, but new parents call us, too. They hear about us from other parents, or they see one of the fliers we sometimes put up around town.

Want to know why the Baby-sitters Club is so successful? Two words: Kristy Thomas. She thought up the idea for the BSC one day when her mom was having trouble finding a sitter. The club started with just Kristy, Claudia, and Mary Anne, but the idea worked so well they had to expand.

We all have titles and duties, like a company. Kristy, of course, is our president. She runs the meetings and thinks up brilliant ideas, such as the record book (which I'll explain later) and the notebook, in which we write about each sitting job. Writing in the notebook is kind of a pain, but it's helpful to read about how other sitters have solved problems with certain kids. (Also, some of the entries are really funny.)

Kid-Kits are another patented Kristy idea. They're boxes filled with old games, toys, and books — basically stuff we found lying around our houses. Sounds boring, huh? Well, kids don't think so. They absolutely *adore* Kid-Kits. Only Kristy could have thought of that. Her brain is so crammed full of stuff, sometimes words just come spilling out of her mouth before she can think. (I guess that's a nice way of saying she can be loud and bossy.)

Guess who's best friends with Kristy the Great and Powerful? Mary Anne the Shy and Meek. They've known each other since they were in diapers. Actually, they sort of look alike. Both are on the short side (Kristy's shorter), and both have dark brown hair and brown eyes. But there the similarities end. Kristy's very athletic. Mary Anne practically breaks out in hives if you mention the word *gym*. Mary Anne's style of dress is neat and preppy. Kristy's style is super-casual and down-to-earth — jeans, T-shirts, sneakers. And that style didn't change one bit after she became rich.

No, she didn't win the lottery. Her mom married this millionaire named Watson Brewer. You see, Kristy grew up across the street from Claudia in a normal, non-rich house. She has two older brothers named Charlie and Sam. When her younger brother, David Michael, was born, her dad took a hike. I mean it. 'Bye-'bye, I'm history, don't-call-me-I'll-call-you. Talk about thoughtless. Well, Mrs. Thomas did a fantastic job raising the kids *and* working full-time. Then she met Watson and — *whoosh!* — off went the Thomas family to live in a mansion. I'm serious, that place is huge. Now it's also pretty crowded. Watson has two kids from his previous marriage (Karen and Andrew), who live there on alternate weekends. Then there's Emily Michelle, an adopted Vietnamese girl. Kristy's grandmother, Nannie, lives there to help run the house, which includes caring for all the pets.

Kristy lives across town now, so her brother Charlie has to drive her to meetings. He always gets her there on time. Kristy is *extremely* punctual, and Charlie knows enough to stay on her good side.

"This meeting will come to order!" Kristy announced as the clock by Claudia's bed turned to 5:30. "Any new business to discuss?"

"Yes," Claudia said. "I made a major discovery." She ran into her closet and disappeared behind a very full rack of clothes.

Mallory Pike gasped. "Uh-oh, a secret

17

world. Like the one in *The Lion, the Witch, and the Wardrobe*."

No such luck. Claudia emerged holding two huge bags that said "Holiday M&M's," decorated in green, silver, and red. "Ta-da!"

"But those are from *last winter*!" Kristy said.

"So?" Claudia replied. "Chocolate doesn't spoil."

I should explain something. Claudia Kishi lives for junk food. She thinks the four food groups are candy, chips, pretzels, and popcorn. If I ever invited her over for Tofu Garden Delight, she'd turn blue and faint. Honestly, I don't know how she stays healthy. And guess what? She has a fabulous figure and her skin doesn't even have the slightest hint of a blemish.

To tell you the truth, Claudia could probably be a model. She's Japanese-American, and she has the most gorgeous almond-shaped eyes and silky black hair. She also has *style* with a capital *S*. She can throw together funky bargain-basement clothes and look sooooo cool.

How someone so stylish can live in such a pig sty of a room is beyond me. There are clothes all over the place. Plus she is an excellent artist, so here's what else is lying around: easels, poster board, jewelry-making tools, paints and brushes, markers, sketch paper, and plaster of paris. Not to mention Ring

Dings, Chunkies, pretzels, Milk Duds, and chips. Claud's room is like a junk food *Where's Waldo?* Her parents are strict about good nutrition and fine literature, so Claudia has to hide all her junk food *and* her Nancy Drew mysteries (she's addicted to them, too). She pulls them out from between sweaters, under her bed, inside shoes, *everywhere*. So it's no surprise that she sometimes loses track of things, like the holiday M&M's.

How do we fit in Claud's room? She manages to shove everything away before meetings. (If she didn't, Kristy would probably nag her forever.)

Anyway, so there we were in Claud's room. Most of us were popping red and green M&M's into our mouths and getting into the holiday spirit about three months early (or nine months late). But not Stacey McGill and me. However, being a a very thoughtful person, Claudia had squirreled away some sesame crackers for us.

No, Stacey's not on a diet. She's also not a health-food fan like I am. She has diabetes, which means her body can't control the level of sugar in her blood. If she ate too many candy bars she could end up in the hospital. Every day she has to take injections of something called insulin. Can you imagine?

Like me, Stacey moved to Stoneybrook permanently grade after her parents divorced. Also, like me, she's blonde (although a darker shade). Other than those things, we're pretty different. Her clothes are cool and sophisticated (mine are more casual). And she is super-smart in math (I'm not).

The math part is the reason Stacey became our club treasurer. She collects dues from us every Monday and puts them in our official treasury (an old manila envelope). Dues are the only *bad* thing about the BSC, but they're necessary. They help pay Claud's phone bill and Charlie Thomas's driving fee. They also buy supplies for Kid-Kits, and pizza for us (if there's a surplus).

Stacey grew up in New York City. I don't know how she did it. The last time I visited I was petrified to leave the apartment I was staying in. I was convinced I'd be mugged, flattened by a falling brick, or attacked by an army of giant cockroaches. Well, somehow Stace lived her life there and turned out pretty normal. After moving to Stoneybrook, her family actually moved *back* to NYC (both moves were because of her dad's job). That was when her parents divorced, and she and her mom moved back here.

I'm so happy Stace is in the BSC. She's easy to talk to, and she's the only member who understands what a divorce feels like. But I

20

have to admit I envy her sometimes. She's only a short train ride away from *her* dad.

"Um, Jessi?" Mary Anne said after carefully swallowing her M&M's. "Did you say you were going away?"

"Oh. Yeah," Jessi replied. "I'm going to Oakley this weekend to visit Keisha." (Oakley is where Jessi grew up, and Keisha is her cousin.)

"That's great," Claudia said. "You haven't been back in — "

"Months!" Jessi was smiling so hard I thought her cheeks would break. "I am totally excited. I can't wait to see Keisha, and I'm going to try to see some of my friends. I'm dying to visit my old ballet school, too. My teacher's going to be shocked to see me."

Mary Anne was entering Jessi's trip in the BSC record book, in her neat handwriting. She's the club secretary, which is *the* hardest job. She keeps track of our sitting schedules, making sure to remember all our conflicts — doctor and orthodontist appointments, ballet classes, and after-school activities. Plus she constantly has to update our client list, complete with current rates (they vary from client to client). On top of *that* she keeps a detailed description of the likes and dislikes of all our charges.

Know how many mistakes she's made? Zero. And knowing her, she probably never will.

Jessi, by the way, is really into ballet. You should see her perform. Incredible! She practically glides in the air. She takes lessons in Stamford and has danced major roles in various productions. Someday she's going to be a pro. And you heard it here first.

I can't mention Jessi without mentioning Mallory Pike. They're best friends, and our junior members. *Junior* because they're eleven years old and in sixth grade, two years younger than the rest of us. They both have early curfews, so they mainly take on afternoon jobs. Here's what they have in common: they love to read (especially horse books), they're convinced their parents treat them like babies, they're the oldest kids in their families, and they're extremely creative. Mallory's talents are writing and illustrating. She wants to be a children's book author someday.

Here's what they don't have in common: Jessi's black and Mal's white, Mal wears glasses and braces (Jessi doesn't), and Jessi has a *much* smaller family than Mal's. There are eight Pike kids altogether (yes, *eight*). Jessi has only two siblings: an eight-year-old sister named Becca and a baby brother named John

Philip Ramsey, Jr. (Squirt, for short).

We have two associate members, Logan Bruno (yes, Mary Anne's boyfriend) and Shannon Kilbourne. They're our backups when we get busy. They don't come to most meetings, but they're both *excellent* sitters. Shannon is the only member who doesn't go to SMS. She goes to a private school, Stoneybrook Day School.

Then there's me. I'm the alternate member. That means I take over whenever anyone can't make a meeting. I became the club treasurer when Stacey moved back to New York. (Boy, was I glad she returned to Stoneybrook.)

Back to the meeting. The more Jessi talked about seeing her old friends, the more my heart sank. Don't get me wrong. I was glad she was so excited, but it made me think of *my* old friends in California.

Then Stacey talked about how much *she* loves to visit *her* old friends.

I kept picturing a map of the United States in my head. I saw a dot marked STONEYBROOK with three lines sticking out from it. One short line connected it to New York City, another short one connected it to Oakley, New Jersey — and a humongously long one stretched clear across to my dad's house in Palo City, California.

23

"You guys are lucky to be so close to your old neighborhoods," I finally said. "I miss mine so much."

Clunk. That stopped the conversation flat.

Kristy spoke up first. "Well, what can you do about it?"

Change the subject, that's what. And hope that someday Kristy would develop plans for a magic carpet or something. "Oh, I'm going there for Thanksgiving," I replied with a shrug. Then I said, "Anyone read about Run for Your Money?"

"Our family already entered!" Kristy said.

"I read that athletics can be harmful for your health," Claudia remarked, stuffing a Ring Ding in her mouth. "But we're going to go anyway. Probably just to watch Janine win all the IQ games." (Claudia's sister, Janine, is a certified genius.)

"I hope they have pinball machines," Mallory said.

"I hope they have foosball," Stacey added.

Claudia looked at her. "What?"

"You know, a table with these long poles attached to players, who kick a ball when you rotate the pole."

"Table hockey!" Mallory said.

"Whatever," Stacey replied.

"Well, you can all cheer me and Charlie in

the three-legged race," Kristy added.

It turned out all my friends' families were going to enter. That was cool. It gave me something to look forward to in the long trudge toward Thanksgiving.

CHAPTER 3

"Oh, this is absurd!" Richard was struggling with his zipper on his pants. "And where am I supposed to drop this?"

None of us could answer. We were *sick* with laughter, sprawled out on the grass of our yard.

It was Saturday morning, and we were practicing for Run for Your Money. Now, if you told me an alien had landed in my backyard, I *probably* wouldn't believe you. But if you told me Richard Spier would agree to participate in an underwear race in Run for Your Money, I'd think you were crazy.

Well, that was exactly what Mom had managed to do — convince Richard. Don't ask me how. She had even bought him a Simpsons tank top undershirt and an oversized pair of boxer shorts with red hearts on them, just for the occasion.

The hearts showed through his pants, which made us laugh even more. Plus his belly jiggled beneath his undershirt.

"I'm really not sure about this. . . ." Richard was now hopping on one foot, trying to pull his pants over his big, clunky shoes. His face was redder than the hearts.

"You look so *sweet*, Richard!" Mom blurted out, still clutching her stomach.

She was wearing lightweight long johns. I was down to a two-piece bathing suit. Mary Anne was wearing a modest one-piece with a skirt.

I should probably explain. In an underwear race you peel off your clothes as you run. The first person to get to the finish line in his or her underwear wins. (It doesn't have to be actual underwear. Mom says people sometimes wear outrageous things. It's the spirit that counts — the spirit of silliness and fun.)

"Oh, honestly, I give up," Richard finally said in a huff. He was standing there in his heart boxers, with his pants gathered around his ankles and his clodhopper shoes poking out. We were *screaming*. We couldn't help it.

Richard was not amused. He started trying to walk back to the house — and you can imagine what that looked like.

That was when he gave up. He just sat on

the ground and started chuckling. "You don't
suppose there's another event we might try to
enter instead?" he asked.

"*No!*" Mary Anne and I replied.

"Waaaaiit!" said Mom. "What about tug-of-
war? We have a rope, don't we?"

"Oooh, great!" Mary Anne said.

"I'll get it," I volunteered.

As I ran into the barn, Richard stood and
began hiking up his pants in a major hurry.
So fast, in fact, that he pushed the heart boxers
upward so they bunched over the top of his
belt.

I found a rope on the barn wall, grabbed it,
and ran out. "How should we do this?" I
asked.

"Girls against boys," Mom said.

Richard looked at her blankly. "Girls
against — "

"Or is that going to be too tough for you,
dear?"

"Too tough? We'll see about that!" Richard
took one end of the rope and walked away
from us, his boxers billowing over the top of
his pants.

I don't know how we kept from cracking
up. Instead, we all dug in until the line was
taut.

"Ready?" Mom announced. "Set? Go!"

"Wait, I — " Richard seemed suddenly uncomfortable about something, but it was too late. We girls had already begun pulling.

Richard pulled back. He's stronger than I thought. His biceps were bulging.

It was unfair, I know. We had caught him off guard. And there *were* three of us. He began staggering forward, losing his balance. And it soon became clear why he'd been uncomfortable. His pants were slipping down again.

"Heave . . . *ho!*" Mom grunted. We gave a strong yank, and — *whomp!* — down went poor Richard.

He landed on his hands and knees, his pants down around his thighs.

"Mr. *Spier?*"

We all turned to see Marilyn and Carolyn Arnold staring at Richard. They're identical twins who live around the corner from us. They were dressed in tennis whites, on their way home from a lesson. Their parents were behind them, gently nudging them onward. I could tell the grown-ups were trying hard not to laugh.

Well, you have never seen a grown man spring to his feet faster. He pulled himself together, trying to look nonchalant. "Hello, there," he called out. "The girls sure are giving me a workout. This Run for Your Money is quite a lot of fun."

Oh, was his face red. Mr. Arnold nodded and said, "Yep. Looks like a good time. Maybe we'll enter, too."

Carolyn Arnold shot a glance at her father. "We will?"

"Uh, come on. It's almost lunchtime," Mrs. Arnold said to her daughters.

"Well, see you folks later!" Mr. Arnold called. "Have fun!"

"Oh, we will! Ha, ha!" Richard replied, with a very forced laugh.

Mary Anne was giving her dad a sympathetic look. "Are you okay?" she asked.

Richard raised one eyebrow. "I have an idea for an event. A family wrestling match — *boys against girls!*"

"Aaaaaagh!" we screamed, giggling like crazy as he tore after us. For a few minutes we all dodged him. I could tell he was loosening up and having a good time.

Before long we all collapsed on the ground, panting. Mom nuzzled up against Richard, who gave her a kiss on the forehead. Then he looked at Mary Anne with a fond smile and put his arm around her shoulders. "I expect the Arnolds will be trying to move to another neighborhood soon," he remarked. "To get away from their weird neighbors."

Mom and Mary Anne laughed. They both

looked happy. Richard looked happy, too.

Me? I was staring at the grass. I *wasn't* feeling happy. I should have been. It was a gorgeous day, warm and summery. We were having a great time. But something was wrong.

At first I couldn't figure out what. Then a weird memory popped into my head. It was a TV show I'd seen, about how computers could completely change photographs by replacing images. You could, like, put yourself in a photo from the Civil War.

Well, when I looked at Richard I imagined putting my dad in his place. And me in Mary Anne's.

And maybe throw in a beach and some smog in the background.

My California homesickness was getting worse by the day. And it made me feel sooo guilty. I mean, I love my life in Stoneybrook, with my mom and my friends. Richard was always sweet to me. Mary Anne was the best sister I could imagine having.

So I didn't want to say anything. Everyone was having a fabulous time that day, and it wouldn't be right to burst the bubble.

"Dawn?" Mary Anne said gently. "What's wrong?"

"I want to go home!" The words just tumbled out of my mouth. I couldn't hold them back.

Fssssssht! The bubble was burst. Richard's smile faded, and he glanced at Mom. Mary Anne shifted herself so she could sit next to me.

I hung my head lower and played with a few strands of grass.

"You've been thinking about your dad and Jeff a lot lately," Mary Anne said.

I nodded. I could barely force the word "Yes" out.

Mom sighed. "Well, I suppose I should call Dad and figure out a good weekend for a visit. It'll be hard to get tickets, you know — "

"I don't mean *go back*, like, go back for a weekend," I interrupted. "I mean really go back. To stay. For six months or so."

"A few months?" Mom looked shocked.

Even I was surprised at what I'd said. But it was true. I just hadn't wanted to admit it. Not even to myself.

My stomach was flopping all around. Not to mention my brain. I had no idea what was going to come out of my mouth now. "I — I just miss my old life, Mom. I can't help it. I miss my friends, the weather . . . but mostly I miss Dad and Jeff. I mean, I've been living away from them for so long."

"I thought you liked it here," Mom protested.

"I do! I *love* it. But I have two families. I love my Stoneybrook family. Really. But I love my California family, too."

"And you want equal time," Mom said.

"Well, I don't know about *equal* — "

"Then what do you mean?"

"I don't *know* what I mean! I just want to be with them, that's all."

I couldn't believe it. Mom looked hurt, almost angry.

Richard spoke up. "I can understand your feelings, Dawn," he said. "It must be hard to be split between your parents."

"But what about school?" Mom barged on. "You'll have to register in a new place, and start in the middle of the year — "

"Yes, very difficult to do," Richard said in a soft voice. "Obviously this is something we need to think carefully about."

"That's okay," I said. "I don't want to upset everybody."

Mom exhaled and shook her head. "I don't mean to sound so negative, sweetheart. It's just that — well, it was so hard to see Jeff go back. And now you . . . I — I've tried my best. Is something bothering you here, something we might be able to work out?"

"Oh, Mom, it's not *you*," I replied.

"Of course it's not," Richard said, giving Mom a hug.

"Okay." Mom was trying very hard to smile.

Boy, did I feel bad. I didn't think Mom would take it so personally. "Well, I know the arrangements would be a lot of work," I said, "and if it's too much, I'll understand." (You don't know how hard it was for me to say those words.)

"Let me think about it, sweetheart," Mom replied. "I can tell how much you want to go."

Mary Anne hadn't said a word through all of this. I looked over at her and realized why. She'd been trying not to cry.

"Oh, Mary Anne," I said. "I'm not going forever."

"I . . ." *Sniff, sniff.* "I know. I'm sorry. I — I want you to be happy, Dawn. Really. It's just that if you go I'll miss you so m — " *Sniff, sniff.* "Much!"

"Well, dears, it's still a big if," Mom said.

Richard rose to his feet. "What do you say we try that tug-of-war again, then go get some pizza for lunch?"

"Great idea," I said.

Mary Anne wiped her eyes. "Sure."

Mom walked to the rope and picked it up. She was smiling at me. I think it was the saddest smile I've ever seen.

CHAPTER 4

Saturday

Kristy, I dont know how you do it. I mean, organising kids, like with Kristys' Crushers. It' so hard. Well, any way, I tryed to do it today. I sat for Jammie and Lucy Newton, and it seemd like a perfict day to practis for Run for Youre Money. Well all I can say is I am so glad I had some help. If I didnt', I think I'd have cullap colexsd or pased out....

"Ba ba ba ba ba ba ba," said Lucy Newton, looking up at Claudia.

"Oops, here's your baba," Claudia replied, gently reinserting a bottle that had fallen from Lucy's mouth.

"Seven!" Jamie Newton called out. "Did you see me, Claudia? Seven!"

"Mm-hm," Claudia said, smiling. "Great, Jamie."

Jamie was perched on his bike with training wheels. He had just completed his seventh round trip on the Newtons' driveway — his seventh very sloooow round trip.

It was early Saturday afternoon. Several blocks away, the Drama of Homesick Dawn was going strong. But at the Newtons' house, Claudia was having a peaceful time, sitting for two of our oldest charges.

Maybe *oldest* isn't the right word. Jamie's four and Lucy's not even one. What I mean is, the Newton kids were among our *first* charges. In fact, Kristy, Claudia, and Mary Anne sat for Jamie before Lucy was born (and before the BSC was invented).

"Eight!" Jamie shouted.

"Great," Claudia said.

"I didn't fall!"

"I know."

"Are you watching?"

"Yes."

Claudia is patient, kind, and cheerful. But even Claudia has limits.

She was going crazy.

She unfolded a copy of the *Stoneybrook News*, which was full of articles about Run for Your Money. She tried to read it, but Jamie screamed out a new number in the middle of each sentence.

At "Thirteen!" Claudia had her big idea.

She remembered that Stacey was sitting for Charlotte Johanssen nearby, and that Jessi and Mal were at the Pikes' house. Run for Your Money would be a perfect excuse to get them together (and get Jamie off the bike). She figured a lot of families would be entering, so everyone could use some practice.

"I'll be right back!" Claudia called out, rushing inside with Lucy. "Stay away from the street!" As she made her phone calls, Jamie charged ahead to Round Trip Eighteen.

Well, Jessi, Mal, and Stacey both *loved* the idea. Claudia felt so relieved, she decided to reward herself. So she took a Milky Way bar from her shoulder bag and tossed it into the Newtons' freezer. She planned to enjoy the FMW (frozen Milky Way) that night.

By the time Stacey, Charlotte, and Becca came charging up the driveway, Jamie was on his thirty-ninth round trip, and Claud was on a lounge chair, busily reading about the rules and events in Run for Your Money. (Lucy had had enough. She was sleeping in an outdoor crib.)

"Forty!" Jamie said. "Forty times up and down the driveway!"

"Yea, Jamie!" Stacey cheered.

Don't encourage him! was what Claudia wanted to say. But she didn't. "Um, you guys feel like practicing for this Run for Your Money thing?" (Okay, not exactly inspiring, but hey, Claud's not an athlete.)

"Yeeeeeahh!" Char and Becca cried.

"No-o-o-o!" Jamie protested.

"Can Becca and I run a three-legged race?" Charlotte wanted to know.

"A three-legged race?" Jamie said. He looked horrified — but interested.

"Sure!" Claudia said. "Come over, Jamie. I'll explain it."

Success. Jamie decided to join in. Stacey ran into the Newton house to get some rope. Becca and Charlotte grinned at Lucy.

And that was when a herd of wildebeests stampeded up the driveway.

Well, that's what it sounded like. Actually, it was Jessi, Mal, and the Pike kids. But that's nine people altogether. Nine *loud* people.

"HI!" they called.

"Waaaaah!" Lucy shrieked.

"I found some rope!" Stacey shouted cheerfully, from the doorway.

"Oooh, a bike!" said Claire Pike, climbing onto Jamie's two-wheeler.

"Nooooooo!" Jamie roared. He ran to Claire and pushed her off.

"Owwwwww!" Claire cried.

It took some serious baby-sitting skills to clear up this situation. Claudia fed Lucy, Stacey separated Jamie and Claire, and Jessi and Mal kept the rest of the Pikes out of trouble.

(As I mentioned before, Mal has seven siblings. There are ten-year-old triplets — Adam, Byron, and Jordan. Then there's Vanessa, who's nine. She wants to be a poet, so she likes to speak in rhyme. Nicky is eight, but wants desperately to be ten like his brothers. Next is seven-year-old Margo, followed by Claire, who's five.)

When everyone was finally quiet, Claudia said, "Okay, there are a lot of events to choose from. You'll all be on the same team. In each event, a team from Stoneybrook plays a team from Lawrenceville, okay?"

"The whole *team* ties their legs together?" Nicky asked.

"That's hard," Margo said.

Adam groaned. "I guess you guys took your *moron* pills this morning."

"Listen up," Claudia replied. "In something

like the three-legged race, the officials will record the time it takes each pair to finish. Then they add up the times to find which *team* was fastest. Now, let's start by practicing some events, then splitting into teams for a mock competition, okay?"

About halfway through the explanation, the kids began tying their legs together, in pairs: Adam-Jordan, Mal-Jessi, and Jamie-Claire (who became the Red team); and Byron-Nicky, Vanessa-Margo (who were the Blue team with Becca and Char). Stacey helped each pair tie one person's right leg to the other's left. (Adam and Jordan had refused help, and they ended up tying their right legs together.)

Claudia had the easy job. She sat in a lounge chair, held Lucy, and watched.

The kids began to practice. Jamie and Claire fell before they moved an inch. Mal and Jessi took it slow, but Jessi kept pointing her toes, which made Mal giggle, so they collapsed. Char and Becca couldn't stay upright, so they decided to crawl. Byron and Nicky yelled at each other but couldn't figure out how to move. Adam and Jordan kept running around in circles, laughing their heads off.

Claudia was giggling so hard, she almost dropped Lucy.

The kids kept at it for awhile. Then they split into teams and held a race. Four pairs were actually able to reach the finish line, in this order: Becca-Char (Blue), Adam-Jordan, Jessi-Mal (both Red), and Byron-Nicky (Blue).

Well, Jordan was steaming. "You stepped in front of us!" he shouted at Becca and Char.

"Did not!" Becca replied.

"No fair," Byron mumbled, his eyes almost tearful. "Jessi and Mal are *sitters*, not kids."

"Yeah!" Adam shouted. "I call a do-over!"

"Guys, it's only a game," Stacey insisted.

"Uh, let's move on to something else," Claudia said, frantically reading the newspaper article. "How about a . . . rolling race?"

This time the kids had to *roll* to the finish line in pairs — holding hands, with heads pointed toward each other and feet pointing outward. Since the yard is pretty small, they did it two pairs at a time. (Mal and Jessi tactfully stayed out of it.)

You can imagine what that was like. Byron and Nicky rolled into the Newtons' garden and squashed three flowers. Becca and Charlotte rolled into each other. Jamie and Claire managed to knock over the bike and get into another fight.

In the middle of the practice, Mrs. Barrett walked by with her three kids. Instantly the older ones, Buddy and Suzi, replaced Jessi and Mal on the Red team.

After a few tries, most of the kids finally

figured out the rolling. Stacey organized them into races, and Adam and Jordan won. They were the fastest.

"No fair!" Margo shouted. "They're bigger!"

"Yeah," Nicky said. "We should get a handicap."

"But you'll be racing on the same team," Stacey reminded them. "This is only a practice."

"Uh, how about the leap frog race?" Claudia called out.

Well, everyone knew how to play leap frog. The teammates lined up and leap frogged in turn till someone reached the finish line.

When the Blue team won, there was an explosion. "Buddy didn't jump with both feet!" Becca screamed.

"Did too!" Buddy protested.

Even Charlotte was upset. "You did not! You cheated."

"Well, Vanessa did the same thing!" Jordan yelled.

"Liar liar, pants on fire!" Vanessa cried.

"I don't want to be in this stupid thing," Buddy said.

"Yeah," Jamie agreed. "I want to ride my bike."

"Run for Your Money silly-billy-goo-goo," Claire mumbled.

Claudia, Stacey, Jessi, and Mal shared a

Look. "What about making up our own events?" Claudia suggested. "Silly stuff, like, I don't know. . . ."

"Water-bomb!" Adam bellowed.

"What's *that*?" Margo asked.

"It's like hot potato," Adam said. "Only you use a water balloon. Whoever lets it break is out."

"We have balloons in the kitchen cupboard!" Jamie shouted.

"Wait!" Claudia called out. "We can't do this without bathing suits!"

"*We're* wearing them already!" Adam exclaimed. "We were going to go to the pool."

"I'll get mine!" Jamie said, running inside.

"No fair!" Buddy complained.

"Let's go see if we can find some rain gear inside," Jessi suggested.

"Yeah!" squealed the Barrett kids.

As they ran indoors with Jessi, the Pike kids stripped to their suits.

"Stacey, can you keep an eye on Lucy for a minute?" Claudia asked.

"Sure."

Claudia raced inside and found the balloons. She filled four of them in the kitchen sink (not too full) and brought them out. Buddy and Suzi followed, dressed in ponchos, with Jessi close behind.

The teams lined up and Claudia threw the

first balloon in the air. Up it went, all wobbly-looking. And down it came — on Nicky's head.

Splooosh! "Owwww!"

The triplets exploded with laughter. Claudia was sure Nicky would burst into tears. But he said "Oops" and started laughing, too.

The second balloon ended up watering the next-door neighbors' lawn. The third rolled under Charlotte's leg, where it — well, died a wet death. The fourth actually stayed in the air a long time, at least six or seven passes.

Next came the race of the giants. Each "giant" was a little kid perched on the shoulders of a big kid, with beach towels or old tablecloths wrapped around each pair so they looked like one huge person.

Jamie's big idea was the "Baby Jester" contest. Whoever made Lucy laugh the most was the winner. Lucy *loved* that — until Buddy's turn. His idea of jesting was a frantic dance, with a frozen grin, flailing legs, and some authentic war screams.

Lucy was horrified. The contest ended then and there.

Oh. There was one other event. Teddy bear volleyball. That had ended with little mounds of white cotton stuffing all over the yard, along with a limp Paddington skin.

A destroyed yard. A traumatized infant. Eleven children with wet clothing. It was one of Claudia's toughest (and most fun) jobs.

Well, at least there was that frozen Milky Way to look forward to.

CHAPTER 5

I had never heard Richard laugh so hard. His face was red. When he hung up the phone, he sat down at the dinner table and said, "That was Jack Arnold. After seeing us this morning, the twins *insisted* he join the underwear race. So the Arnolds went out and bought boxers for him."

"Did they get those cute heart ones?" Mom asked.

"Nope," Richard said. "Huge pictures of Garfield. See what we started?"

Mary Anne put her hand over her mouth and giggled.

I laughed, too, even though the thought of Mr. Arnold in Garfield boxer shorts wasn't all that hilarious to me.

I was being very, very good. I was making sure to seem happy, cheerful, and pleasant. I had already ruined the morning, and I was determined not to talk about California for the rest of that Saturday.

We'd ordered out for Chinese food that night, which is one of my favorite things to do. The meal was fantastic, and at the end we opened fortune cookies.

" 'You will inherit a great deal of money,' " Mom read. "Hey, great! Dinner's on me."

Richard looked up with a dry, disappointed expression. " 'A handsome stranger will enter your life.' "

" 'Success is one per cent inspiration and ninety-nine per cent perspiration,' " Mary Anne read. "Yuck."

I stared at my fortune. I couldn't believe what it said.

Have you ever had a psychic experience? You know, spirits and ESP and things like that? Well, I know that stuff is real — and I was getting a signal.

I cleared my throat, then read, " 'You will be going on a long journey to a faraway place.' "

There was a silence. I'm sure it lasted a split-second, but it felt like a *long* time.

"Well," Richard said finally. "Sounds . . . exotic."

"These things are so silly," I lied.

"Okay, whose turn to do the dishes?" Mom asked quickly.

"Mine!" I jumped up from the dinner table.

I grabbed my plate and carried it to the sink. "Thanks!" I said cheerfully to each family member who dumped a plate on the counter. As I loaded the dishwasher, Mary Anne wandered in and began sponging off the counters. Richard and Mom were bustling around in the dining room.

"That was so *weird*," Mary Anne whispered.

"Hm?"

But I knew what she meant. And she knew I knew. When Richard walked in carrying a stack of empty takeout cartons, Mary Anne just gave me a Look. A "We'll talk later" Look.

After I finished loading the dishwasher, we ran up to my bedroom and closed the door.

It was Mary Anne who spoke first. "I guess it's really going to happen, isn't it?"

"I thought I was the only one who believed in fortunes," I said.

Mary Anne shrugged. "Well . . . I do, too, sometimes. Logan once got one that said he would reach his most desired goal, and the next day he scored a touchdown." I looked at her blankly, and she said, "You have to go over the *goal* line to score. See?"

I plopped down on my bed. I couldn't hold it back anymore. The words just gushed out. "Oh, Mary Anne, I hope it *is* true. I mean, I don't want to upset you or anything, but I feel so . . . cut off. I want to be there if my dad decides to marry Carol. I want to really spend time with Jeff. I mean, I know he can be a pain, but I love him."

I had to be careful talking about Jeff. He visited us a while ago, and it was *not* a fabulous time. Jeff and Richard didn't get along, then Mary Anne got angry at Jeff, then I got angry at *her*. . . . What a mess.

"It's okay," Mary Anne said gently. "I think you should go."

"You do?"

Mary Anne nodded. "Yes. I've been thinking about it. Of course I'll miss you a lot. But if you stay, you're just going to feel sad. And seeing you like that would be terrible." She bowed her head and said softly, "Besides, six months isn't *so* long."

"Oh, Mary Anne. I promise I'll write every day — "

I stopped. What was I talking about? No one had given me permission to go. There I was, all excited, and the whole thing was just a dream.

"Anyway," I continued. "we shouldn't talk about it. What if Mom says no?"

"What about your dad?" Mary Anne asked. "Have you told him how you feel?"

"Well, no, not exactly."

"Why don't you call him? He would have to be part of this decision, too."

"I guess, but . . . I don't know. If I ask *his* permission, and I haven't even gotten Mom's, that would be like going behind her back."

"I don't mean ask permission. Not now. Just *talk*, Dawn. Tell him how torn up you feel. You can't just keep this inside."

Leave it to Mary Anne. When it comes to emotional things, she always knows what to do.

I took a deep breath. I looked at the clock. It was 8:27, which meant 5:27 in California. Dad and Jeff would probably be home. If I didn't call now, I might chicken out.

"Okay." I stood up and walked to the top of the stairs. "Mom?" I called. "I'm going to use the phone!"

"Okay, sweetheart!" she called back. I could hear the TV blaring some classical music. Probably one of Richard's beloved simulcasts, those concerts they broadcast on TV and radio at the same time. I knew I'd be safe for at least an hour.

"Good luck," Mary Anne said, slipping away to her room.

"Thanks." I walked into Mom and Richard's bedroom and closed the door. I still felt a little sneaky, but I had already made my decision.

Sitting down on the bed, I picked up the phone and tapped out my dad's number.

"Helllll-*lo!*" sang a sweet and chipper female voice.

My stomach tied itself in a knot. It was definitely *not* the voice I'd expected.

"Carol?" I said.

"Yes! Who is this?"

"Uh, Dawn. Dawn Schafer."

"Well, hello, Dawn *Schafer!*" Carol laughed. "Did you think I'd forgotten your last name?"

I couldn't figure out why that was so funny. "No, I — "

"How *are* you? Oh, wow. This is so cool. I was just thinking about you."

Oh, wow? So cool? I had to shake my head. This was a thirty-two-year-old I was talking to. "Really? I'm fine. And you?"

"Great. I'm making a fancy salad — radicchio, edible flowers, sun-dried tomatoes. You should see it! Oh, your dad will be so happy to hear you called! I better give the phone to him. Besides, I have olive oil and lemon juice all over my fingers. When are we going to *see* you?"

"Well, I — "

"Oops, here he is! He's taking the phone out of my hand. Oops! *'Bye, Dawn!*"

" 'Bye!" I said.

(I thought I liked Carol. Maybe I was wrong.)

"Heyyy, how's my Sunshine?" Dad greeted me.

"Hi, Dad!" I felt all my gloominess wash away. I wish you could hear my dad's voice. It's so deep and laid-back and comforting. Honestly, I think he could have been a TV announcer. "Do you have a few minutes to talk?"

"For you? As long as you want!"

We chatted for a minute. Then, taking a deep breath, I said, "Dad, um . . . I've been thinking really hard about how much I miss California."

"Yeah. But you know, honey, I think Connecticut is one of the most beautiful — "

"Well, not California, exactly, but *you*. And Jeff. And my friends. And even Mrs. Bruen." (She's my dad's housekeeper.) "What I mean is, I really want to move back for awhile. Like for a few months. I'm not asking *permission*. I just want to know what you think."

"What do I think? Well — I — Dawn, are you sure about this?"

Gulp. I felt as if I were on an elevator that had just dropped ten floors. Dad was supposed to sound *thrilled* — or at least a little positive.

"Yeah, I'm sure," I said. I explained all my reasons, and he listened silently.

At the end, I could hear him sigh. "How does your mom feel about it?"

"Not too great."

"Mm, I wouldn't think so. I mean, with Jeff already out here."

"You don't sound too happy, either, Dad." I was fighting the urge to cry.

"Oh, Dawn, I'd be *overjoyed* if you came. Don't get me wrong. It's just that . . . well, I hope you're not setting yourself up for disappointment. It's not easy going back to a place after you've left."

"I know, but I don't want to *move* back. It would just be temporary."

Dad was silent for a long time. Finally he said, "I suppose I should talk with your mom."

"Mom?" I was mortified. "But — she doesn't — she'll think — "

"Don't worry. I'll explain everything. I'll say you called only to *discuss* the idea, not to make me side with you against her. Okay?"

"Okay. I'll go get her."

I ran out of the room. Mary Anne was peering from her doorway with huge, questioning eyes. I smiled and ran downstairs.

Mom was practically asleep, watching some old bearded man conduct an orchestra full of younger bearded men and unbearded women. "Mom?" I said.

"Huh?"

"Dad's on the phone. Can you talk to him?"

Mom looked a little — well, annoyed, shocked, scared, wary, you name it. She picked up the extension in the kitchen. "Hello?"

I pretended I had things to do downstairs. I walked around the living room. Then I wiped off the clean dining room table. Then I inspected the dishwasher.

I heard snatches of conversation: ". . . midterm enrollment . . . after-school activities . . . statewide achievement standards . . . *sure* I feel that way. I'm human . . . six months . . . you think so? . . . That would be nice . . . so sad lately. . . ."

It was a looooong conversation. My imagination was going wild dreaming up ways to make myself look busy. By the time Mom hung up, I was examining the front hall carpet.

I ran into the kitchen. "Well?" I said. "Did you talk about it?"

I expected Mom's face to look all grumpy and thoughtful. But she gave me a warm smile. "Sure we did. It's the *only* thing we talked about. Give us some time, Dawn. It's a big change. We're going to sleep on it and talk again tomorrow. Okay?"

"Okay, sure," I said. I nodded and went upstairs. I was cool. I was reasonable. I walked straight to my room. I shut the door behind me.

Then I buried my face in my pillow and screamed at the top of my lungs.

Mary Anne came running in. "Did they say yes?"

"No," I said, grinning.

"Then why were you screaming?"

"They didn't say no. And Mom wasn't angry!"

Mary Anne looked at me as if I were crazy. "Uh, okay. I guess that's progress."

"Yup," I said.

Mary Anne gave me another curious look, then went back to her homework.

Me? I guess I was happy to have the matter out in the open. I was sure that if I stuck to my guns, I had a chance.

And all I needed was a chance.

CHAPTER 6

"Yes, it is early in the school year, but I'm not sure you understand," Mom was saying into the phone.

It was Sunday afternoon. Mom and Dad were talking for the second time that day. Their earlier conversation had been horrible. Mom had been crabby, and obviously Dad hadn't been any better. Fortunately, they seemed to be pretty calm now.

Mary Anne was off sitting for the Kuhns, and Richard was food shopping, so I had to face the tension alone. What do I like to do to relieve tension? Talk on the phone! Doesn't it figure? So instead, I decided to read a mystery — in the living room, conveniently within earshot of the kitchen.

"They're already a few weeks into the curriculum," Mom continued. "Yeah, I guess I should ask Mrs. Amer."

Whoa. This was a big breakthrough. Mrs.

Amer is my guidance counselor. So Mom and Dad were no longer talking about whether I *should* go, but how I would adjust if I *did* go!

I pulled myself together. A real "yes" was still a long way off. I knew I should remain calm, calm, calm.

"Okay, what else?" Mom said. "Yes, she does date . . . occasionally. Steady? Well, no, but there is a boy she writes to pretty often."

I blushed. That boy is Logan Bruno's cousin, Lewis. We had a great time when he visited, but we're more pen pals than anything now.

"Yes," Mom continued. "She has to be home by nine on weekdays and ten on weekends, unless she's sitting late. . . . *Baby*-sitting. . . . Clothes? Uh, yes, she picks them out herself. She's thirteen, you know."

Hmm. Dad was asking some pretty serious questions — some pretty dumb ones, too. I guess he was just trying to find out all he could about my life now. Visits are one thing, but Dad was going to have to be a parent to a teenaged girl.

Maybe. *Maybe.* I had to take things one step at a time.

When Mom hung up, I debated running into the kitchen. But before I could make up my mind, I heard her tapping out another number.

"Hi, Linda. It's Sharon Spier. I just need to

know the going rates for coach airfare to Los Angeles. . . . I don't have a date yet. How far in advance do flights book up? . . . Uh-huh, right. . . . Well, thanks a lot. . . . Okay, 'bye."

Airfare? My jaw almost hit the floor. I flew into the kitchen. Mom was scribbling something on a pad of paper.

"Mom?" I squeaked.

She smiled knowingly. "Just checking things out. Airfares are so crazy these days."

"But those things you and Dad were talking about. . . ."

"You weren't supposed to hear that!" Mom laughed. "We'll discuss it over dinner with the whole family."

"*Over dinner?* Come on, Mom. That's not fair. I'm dying to know what happened! What did Dad say? You decided something, didn't you? Otherwise you wouldn't want to talk about it with the whole family! Right? Oh, please please please tell me."

Mom kept smiling, although I thought I could see tears in her eyes. "Okay. Sit down, sweetheart, before you fly through the window."

I sat.

"We just don't know whether or not the Palo City school is teaching the same things as SMS," she began. "If not, you could end up terribly bored *or* terribly lost. Now, I need to talk to Mrs. Amer tomorrow, and your dad's going to talk to a guidance counselor out there — "

"And if they say it's all right?" I butted in.

"Well, *if* they convince us that you'll be able to cope with the change, then yes, we'll let you go for six months."

I rocketed out of my chair and threw my arms around her. "Ohhhhh! You are the *best*, wonderfulest, understandingest mom in the universe!"

"Honey, please don't get your hopes up yet," Mom said gently. "Let's wait to hear what your counselor says."

"Right." I nodded and stood up. "I understand."

Ding-dong! "Delivery man!"

It was Richard. He pushed open the front door and clomped through the living room, loaded down with four humongous grocery bags. I have no idea how he managed to ring the doorbell.

Mom and I ran out and helped bring in the other bags. They barely fit on the kitchen counter.

"Quite a haul, huh?" Richard said proudly.

Richard shops with a boxful of coupons organized by category. He takes his calculator and makes sure to get only the groceries that are on sale. Then he figures out the percentage he's saved over the regular prices.

Mom and I glanced inside the bags. "Did you remember the acorn squash?" Mom asked.

Richard's smile disappeared. A mistake! I don't know who was more surprised, Richard or Mom and me.

Well, we managed to reassure Richard that he had done a great job shopping. And he did bring us some slices of fabulous prepared lasagna for dinner (vegetarian for me).

While we were eating, Mom broke the news to Mary Anne and Richard about her conversation with Dad. The four of us talked about it then, but only a little. No one wanted to talk about it *too* much until the trip was definite.

Later on Mary Anne and I squirreled away in my room. "I am sooo nervous!" Mary Anne squeaked.

"*You're* nervous?" I said. "How do you think *I* feel? What if Dad calls tomorrow and says the kids out there are studying, like, Ancient Streptococcus or something?"

Mary Anne burst out laughing. "Ancient Streptococcus? What's that?"

"I don't know. I made it up." I began pacing. "Oh, I can't stand this. How am I going to sleep? And what about tomorrow at school? What am I going to tell everybody?"

"Nothing," Mary Anne replied. "There's nothing definite to tell."

"But Kristy's going to want to know right away. Remember when I went to visit Jeff when he was sick? That was only a couple of *weeks*, and it was hard to replace me!"

I realized how conceited that sounded, but Mary Anne understood what I meant.

"But suppose your parents say no, Dawn? Not that I'm wishing that, but just suppose? Then you'll upset everybody for no reason."

I sighed. Mary Anne was right. It was best to keep it quiet.

I was a wreck the next day. Every time I walked by the guidance office I could have sworn they were talking about me. I have no idea what happened in any of my classes — except that during math Alan Gray (the Official SMS Jerk) kept cupping his hands over his mouth and saying, "Come in, Dawn. This is earth. Do you read me?" At lunch I managed to dip my hair in a glass of tomato juice (*very* cool). Claudia helped me clean it off in the girls' room — and I practically exploded from wanting to tell her my secret.

After the final bell, I met Mary Anne in front

of school and we *ran* home. Mom was at work, so I threw my books on the kitchen floor and called her office.

"Good afternoon, Mrs. Ballmer speaking."

"Hi! May I speak to Mrs. Schafer?" I blurted.

"Who?"

"Mrs. . . . Mrs. Spier?"

"No, this is Mrs. *Ballmer*. B-A-L-L — "

"Sharon! Is Sharon Spier there, please?"

"Oh. Uh, just a moment."

I was dying. My stomach felt like a pretzel. I hoped Mrs. Ballmer wouldn't go wandering away and forget about the phone.

"Hello, Sharon Spier here."

"Mom, it's me! Hi! Did you call Mrs. Amer?"

"I sure did — "

"And did you call Dad?"

"Yes, and — "

"Did he call the counselor there?"

"Yes, Dawn — "

"Well, what did they say?"

Mom laughed. "Let me finish a sentence. A couple of the courses you're taking now have a slightly different emphasis in the SMS curriculum."

"You mean they're harder?"

"Well, some harder, some easier, it seems. But the point is, both counselors think you shouldn't have any trouble making up the work — either moving there or moving back here."

"Really?"

"Really."

"So that means I can go?"

"Yes, it does. I booked you a flight for three weeks from this past Saturday."

"*AAAAAAAAAAAAUUUGGHHHHHHH!*" I screamed. "Ooh, sorry!"

"That's okay," Mom said. "I have another ear."

"Oh, Mom, thank you! Thank you! I love you so much. You are the greatest."

"All I can say is, you better write."

"Every day! Twice a day!"

"Well, I'd even accept once a week. Now listen, sweetheart, I have to get back to work. We'll celebrate tonight, okay?"

"Okay. 'Bye!"

" 'Bye."

I slammed the phone down. Mary Anne was standing an inch away from me, grinning like crazy. We threw our arms around each other and *shrieked*.

"I knew it!" Mary Anne said. "Tell me everything."

I repeated what my mom had told me. Mary Anne nodded excitedly

"What a relief!" I said. "Now I can feel like

a human again. I couldn't stand not talking about this!"

"What about the meeting today?" Mary Anne asked. "Are you going to break the news?"

"I guess so. You think I should?"

"Why not?"

"Maybe I should call Claudia in advance so she can hide a cake in her sock drawer or something."

Mary Anne giggled. "Dawn, I'm so happy for you! You're like your old self again."

"California, here I come!" I screamed.

Whoa. Ease up, Dawn, I told myself. I realized I was being totally inconsiderate of Mary Anne's feelings. As if I were happy to be leaving her.

But she just smiled and kept asking me questions about my trip. No tears. Not even a sniffle. She seemed just as happy as I was.

For a moment, just a moment, I wondered whether Mary Anne was really going to miss me.

But I pushed that thought out of my mind. I couldn't wait to tell my friends the news.

CHAPTER 7

"This meeting will come to order!" Kristy barked.

I had sat in Claud's room for five whole minutes without saying a word. I wanted to wait for the perfect moment to break my news.

"Does anyone have any club business?" Kristy asked.

That was it.

"I do!" I called out. "I'm going to be moving back to California for six months!"

Cheers rang out. A brass band clanged through the room. Reporters formed a circle around me.

Well, not exactly. My friends stared at me blankly, as if I'd made my announcement in Swedish.

Finally Stacey asked, "For real?"

I nodded.

"Is this, like, an emergency?" Mallory asked.

"No," I said. Patiently I told my story. I made sure to mention (several times) how much I would miss everybody, and how I would definitely come back when the six months were over.

Finally Stacey looked at me with this warm smile. "Dawn, you sound so happy," she said.

"*But six months?*" Claudia chimed in. "We're going to miss you so much!"

"Yeah!" Jessi, Mal, and Stacey agreed.

Then everyone began talking at once:

"What are you bringing?"

"Is it still swimming weather there?"

"Are you going to have to go to school?" (That was Claudia's question.)

"Send pictures!"

"Send pictures of guys on the beach!"

"Just send the guys!"

Before long we were all giggling. All except Kristy. She was *trying* not to look angry, but she couldn't keep the frown from her face.

"Ahem," Kristy finally said. "Maybe we should talk about the consequences of this?"

Claudia rolled her eyes. "Come on, Kristy. She's not *moving*. She's just going for a visit."

"Right," Kristy replied. "And we'll be short one member for six months. That's twenty-six weeks, times three meetings a week is . . . what, Stacey?"

"Um, seventy-eight," Stacey answered. "But Kristy—"

"Seventy-eight meetings is a lot," Kristy said. "As it is, the seven of us are booked solid. In case you haven't noticed, we've been calling on Logan and Shannon all the time. What's going to happen when we *lose* one member?"

"Kristy, come on — " Claudia began.

"Well, we have to think of these things, right?" Kristy protested. "I mean, I know you miss your dad, Dawn. But six months just seems like a lot."

To tell you the truth, I did feel awful about leaving the club. But I didn't expect Kristy to react that way.

"Kristy," I said, "I'm not doing this to hurt you guys. I wouldn't dream of it. I tried to explain. I *have* to go. It's the most important thing in my life right now."

"Hey, don't worry," Claudia reassured me. "We'll figure out what to do."

Kristy just glared at her.

"Look," I said quickly, "I have thought about this. I know you'll have to replace me temporarily, and I promise I'll help solve the problem before I leave. It's the least I can do."

RINNNNGG!

The sound of the phone was such a relief.

"Hello?" Claudia said, snatching the receiver. "Oh, hi, Mrs. Hobart. . . . Okay, I'll call back in a minute."

She hung up and said to Mary Anne, "A week from Wednesday? Everyone wants a sitter for that day."

Mary Anne nodded. "Parent-teacher conferences at SES." (That's Stoneybrook Elementary School.) She looked up from the BSC record book and said, "Well, we're all busy, but I'm sure Logan wouldn't mind. He loves the Hobart kids. I'll call him if you want."

"I'm sure you will," Claudia said with a sly smile.

"Maybe he'd want to be my replacement while I'm away," I added.

"Logan definitely prefers being an associate," Kristy said. "Besides, remember when we did ask him to be a permanent member? It didn't work out too well."

Kristy was right. Once I'd gone to California for a few weeks when Jeff had gotten sick, and Logan had become a regular member. But apparently Logan's football teammates had made his life horrible with teasing and practical jokes.

"Besides," Kristy added, "if Logan or Shannon became a regular member, then we'd be short an associate member."

"Well, it's better than nothing," I said.

Mary Anne had already gotten through to Logan on the phone. She explained the situation to him, mentioned the Hobart job, and asked if he would replace me. Then her face became very solemn. "Mm-hm . . . I know . . . it must be . . . well, that would help. . . . Uh-huh, I'll tell them. 'Bye."

She hung up and turned to Kristy. "He says he'll sit for the Hobarts, but football practice is getting really intense now, so he couldn't be a regular member."

Oh, well. One down. "I'll call Shannon," I said.

She was home, too. I filled her in and asked her the big question.

"I wish I could," was her response. "But I'm starting this after-school tutoring project, for the honor society. It's going to last at least two months. But maybe after . . ."

Two down.

Kristy wasn't too jolly about the news. "I don't want you to feel guilty, Dawn," she said, "but this is going to be a big mess."

"I'm not so sure about that," Mary Anne spoke up. "I mean, how often is *every single one* of us busy?"

"A week from Wednesday," Kristy quickly replied.

"Krist*yyyy*," Stacey joined in. "That's so rare. We hardly ever have to turn away work.

I think we'll be able to survive without a seventh full member for awhile."

I could tell everyone was avoiding the obvious other possibility. So I brought it up. "What about taking in a new member?" I asked.

"You mean, like, temporarily, while you're gone?" Jessi asked.

"Well . . . yeah," I said.

"Not to *replace* you," Mary Anne added. "We would never do that."

She flashed a glance at Kristy, but Kristy only said, "It's not easy getting new members."

"Dawn was a new member once," Claudia pointed out brightly.

"So were Janet and Leslie," Kristy replied. (Those were two members who didn't work out well, back before I joined the BSC.) "Besides, what do we do with the new person after six months? Kick her out?"

"Look," Stacey said, "we don't have to solve this problem right now. Dawn's not leaving for three weeks. Let's enjoy her while she's here."

"Oh!" Claudia blurted. "I think I have some popcorn rice cakes." She hopped off her bed and started rummaging around in her dresser drawers.

Kristy sighed. "I'm sorry. It's just that we're getting very busy."

As if to prove Kristy's point, the phone began ringing — and it hardly stopped until six o'clock. In between we talked about a few other things, like Run for Your Money preparations and Jessi's upcoming trip to Oakley.

But the mood remained pretty tense. It was hard not to think about my decision and how it affected everybody. Leaving Stoneybrook was getting more complicated than I expected.

CHAPTER 8

Saturday

If you've never been to a big Greek party, you should go. Whoa. You wouldn't believe it. The Papadakises were having a family reunion, and what a family! I mean, Zeus didn't come down with his thunderbolts or anything, but he didn't really need to. The kids provided plenty of fireworks....

Five days had passed since I'd mentioned my trip in the BSC meeting. Kristy was no longer quite so snarly. In fact, she apologized to me and wished me luck.

Now that my trip was a reality, I had started to pack. Well, sort of. I'd opened up a couple of suitcases on my floor and thrown a few clothes in.

The truth? Somehow now I wasn't as excited as I had been. I guess the reality of my trip was sinking in. My head was spinning with questions. Was it selfish to abandon the BSC — and Mom and Mary Anne and Richard — for six months? Why was everyone acting so *upbeat* about my decision lately? Were they secretly glad I was going? What if I hated living in California?

Anyway, while I was pondering these questions, Kristy was helping the Papadakises on the day of their reunion. Mr. Papadakis's two sisters were coming from New York with *their* families. Mrs. Papadakis's two brothers and one sister were coming with *their* families. Plus a bunch of other cousins and aunts and uncles and friends Kristy had never heard of.

Kristy arrived at their house early, to take care of the kids while the Papadakises set up for the party. The Papadakises have a huge yard. There's a basketball court in the driveway and a badminton area by the garage. On this day, behind the house were dozens of card tables, covered with paper tablecloths and disposable place settings. In the air was a pungent, mouth-watering barbecue smell. Mr. Papadakis was putting a tape deck and loudspeakers on the back porch. Kristy approached him to say hi, but something made her stop in her tracks.

Off to the right, at the edge of the woods behind the Papadakises' house, were four barbecue pits in the ground. Above each one was an animal carcass on a rotating spit.

I am so glad I wasn't there. I think I would have tossed my crackers. Kristy, who isn't fazed by much, was a little grossed out, too.

"Delicious, huh?" Mr. Papadakis called out. "Those are lambs, fresh from the farm! You have never tasted anything so tender. Here, let me cut you some before the guests arrive."

"No!" Kristy said, almost shouting. "I mean, maybe later. I had a late breakfast."

"I'll save you some pieces," Mr. Papadakis insisted.

"Hi, Kristy!"

Hannie and Linny came running out of the house. (Hannie's seven and Linny's nine.) They were followed by two-year-old Sari, who toddled out with a little moon-face smile. "Kiss-tee!" she squealed.

"Hello!" Mrs. Papadakis chimed in, backing through the door with two tinfoil-covered trays. She set them on a picnic table and smiled at Kristy. "Our special *spanakopita* and *tiropita*. Want to sneak a piece?"

"Thanks, but I think I'll go play with the kids," Kristy said. She didn't know *what* would be peeking at her from under that foil.

Before long Kristy was really working. Linny fell and cut his knee. Hannie dropped a glass when she went in the kitchen. Sari kept wanting to play near the barbecue pits.

When the guests started to arrive, Mr. Papadakis turned on the tape deck. This loud, exotic music blared out, with a strong beat and a guitarlike instrument, which Mr. Papadakis called a *bouzouki*. (Kristy liked the bouzouki but thought the singers sounded as if they had indigestion.)

Well, the Papadakis family turned out to be absolutely *humongous*. Kristy counted five Nikos, four Alexandras, three Peters, two Marias, two Takis, and a Gus. Fortunately a lot of them were too old to need sitters (including fifteen-year-old Niko who was extremely cute, according to Kristy).

So you can imagine Kristy's surprise when some of the neighborhood kids decided to wander over.

"Linny! Hannie! Hi!" Bill Korman yelled.

He and his sister Melody ran into the yard, all wide-eyed. (Bill's nine and Melody's seven.)

"Uh, guys," Kristy said. "I don't know if Hannie and Linnie have permission — "

"Heyyy! Welcome to the party!" Mr. Papadakis's voice boomed out. He trotted over to Bill and Melody and said, "Are you hungry? Would you like to try some lamb?"

Melody made a face. "Do you have Triscuits?"

"Melody!" Bill scolded. "Be polite."

"Triscuits coming right up!" Mr. Papadakis said, running into the house.

When he returned, with Triscuits *and* Wheat Thins *and* Teddy Grahams, Kristy's brother and stepsiblings appeared.

"Karen! Andrew! David Michael! Good to see you!" Mr. Papadakis said.

"Yum! Teddy Grahams!" Andrew answered. (He's four; Karen and David Michael are seven.)

"Sit and enjoy," Mr. Papadakis went on, putting the boxes on one of the card tables. The kids gathered around like flies around honey.

Eight charges. For any other baby-sitter, that would be a lot. For Kristy, it was an opportunity.

She was looking around, trying to figure out

a way to organize a soccer game, when Linny said, "Hey, Kristy! Can we practice for Run for Your Money?"

Perfect. Even though I'm sure Kristy would have thought of it herself (hrrmph). "Sure!" she said. "What'll we start with?"

"Basketball shooting!" the Korman kids screamed.

"Bang bang!" Sari said.

Linny ran into the garage and got two basketballs. "I shoot first!" he bellowed.

"No way!" David Michael protested. "We're guests!"

"Let's make teams," Kristy suggested. "How about the Papadakises and Andrew against the Kormans and Karen and David Michael — "

"We'll *cream* 'em," Linny said.

Bill stuck out his chest. "No, you won't!"

"Beanpole!" Linny said.

"Cootie head!"

As they argued, a couple of the older cousins grabbed the basketballs and started playing.

After lots of crying and some general pandemonium, Kristy explained Run for Your Money to everyone. Well, the Papadakis cousins loved the idea. The trouble was, they didn't live in Stoneybrook *or* Lawrenceville. But that didn't stop them. After basketball, the kids held a massive three-legged race that ended up almost toppling the food table. Sari wanted to join in, so Kristy tied her leg to a Cabbage Patch doll's leg.

Out came the cameras. I believe Sari will be haunted by pictures of that event for the rest of her life.

Next, Kristy set up a game of horseshoes for the kids. Of course, Linny wanted to take the first turn.

He lifted a horseshoe and began spinning his arm around. "The windup . . ."

"Linny," Kristy warned, "this isn't baseball!"

"And . . . the . . ."

"Linny!" Kristy tried again.

" . . . Pitch!" Linny let go of the horseshoe too late — way too late. The horseshoe went flying toward the house.

"Heads up!" Kristy shouted.

Everyone looked around in confusion. The horseshoe came hurtling downward.

Plop! It landed in a plateful of gooey pastries.

"My baklava!" Mrs. Papadakis yelled.

"Oooops," Linny muttered.

A roar of laughter went up. "Hey, it's good luck!" one of the aunts called out.

After a couple more events, it was naptime for Sari. Then Kristy and the kids ate some food (by the way, she said the lamb *was* delicious, but that's a carnivore for you). After that came dessert and some Greek dancing to wild music. The guests joined hands and snaked around the yard.

By the time the party was over, Kristy was exhausted (yes, Kristy). She said good-bye to the Papadakises and walked home with David Michael, Karen, and Andrew.

I found out *much* later what they talked about after the party — me!

"Kristy?" Karen said. "Are you sad about Dawn?"

Kristy nodded (at least she *said* she did). "Yeah. I'm going to miss her."

"You know what we did when Amanda Delaney moved away?" Karen asked. "I gave her a party. You should do that for Dawn. It was really fun."

"Yeah!" Andrew and David Michael said.

Kristy's eyebrows rose. "Hmmmm. Not a bad idea."

She ran to the phone. First she called Mary Anne, then Mallory, then Claudia, then Stacey. She almost called Jessi, until she realized Jessi was in Oakley for the weekend.

Everyone agreed. The party was a great idea.

And poor little old me didn't know a thing about it.

CHAPTER 9

"Are you sure nothing's wrong?" Kristy said to Jessi.

"*Yes*," Jessi replied. "You've asked me that a million times."

Jessi was exaggerating. Our Monday meeting was only about five minutes old. But she had spent those five minutes under her own little storm cloud. She was sitting on Claudia's floor, staring out the window, her knees drawn up to her chin.

We had already paid our weekly dues and taken a phone call. Claud was busy distributing goodies.

"Claudia, these are absolutely disgusting," Stacey suddenly said, holding up a plastic bag of cookies.

"Yeah?" Claudia took the bag and read it: " 'Chock Full of Chakra Macrobiotic Dessert Snacks . . . active ingredients: comfrey leaves

80

and kelp, sweetened with barley malt and raisin juice.' "

"Ew!" Mallory said.

"What's kelp?" Mary Anne asked.

"Tiny green fish that swim through your bloodstream and eat bacteria," Kristy replied with a straight face.

"Really?" Claudia looked horrified.

Stacey groaned. "Don't listen to her."

Kristy just grinned.

I had to admit, even for a natural-foods freak like me, those cookies were pretty horrible.

Yes, I ate one. In fact, we actually passed them around for a tasting. Have you ever seen anyone turn green? Mary Anne did. Mal refused even to look at them. Claudia scraped off a teeny layer of one with her teeth, and brave Kristy gobbled a whole one down. Then they both devoured a box of Raisinets to get rid of the flavor.

When the bag was passed to Jessi, she didn't notice it at first. She was still staring out the window.

"Here," Kristy said. "Your turn."

Jessi shook her head and waved the bag away.

"Hey, what's up?" Kristy said. "You've been grumpy since you got here."

Jessi made a face and frowned.

Fortunately, Mary Anne decided to use a little more tact. "Jessi, how was your trip?"

Jessi sighed. In a mumbly voice, still looking out the window, she said, "Pretty terrible."

"Uh-oh," Claudia said. "What happened?"

Finally Jessi opened up. "Well, I get there, right? And Keisha has this new haircut and is wearing makeup. We say hi and everybody goes inside for lunch. Then the bell rings and it's this new friend of hers named Jennifer, who is wearing so much perfume I can't breathe. Jennifer says, 'Is she going dressed like *that*?' Meaning me. It turns out they go to the mall every Saturday to hang out, all dressed up."

"And your aunt and uncle let her go, even though she had company?" Stacey asked.

"No," Jessi replied. "They told her she couldn't go, and Jennifer made this face, like they were being soooo horrible. And Keisha got really upset. She and Jennifer whispered things together out on the porch for a half hour while I just sat around. My aunt finally told Keisha to say good-bye and come back in — and then Keisha wouldn't even talk to anyone the whole rest of the afternoon."

"You're kidding," Mary Anne said. "How rude."

"Well, since she was being so weird, *I* asked if I could take a walk to visit my old ballet school. I invited Keisha to go, but she said no. Anyway, it turns out my teacher divorced her husband and moved to Ohio to go to law school or something. The school is now an aerobics center, and the new teacher wouldn't even let me in the door. So *then* I walked by my old house — and they were chopping down these two beautiful maple trees out front. Those were *my* trees! I used to go to sleep on summer nights listening to the leaves rustle outside my bedroom window. Some guy with a chainsaw said the trees were blocking the power lines. So I went back to Keisha's, all upset — and she was mad at me because *I* got to go out and have such a fabulous time."

"Ugh, what a nightmare," Mal said.

"How about Sunday?" Claudia asked.

"After church we had a big roast chicken, and the Raymonds came over. They're old friends of my family."

"Well, *that* sounds nice," Mary Anne said.

"Except for the fact that Neil Raymond, their son, who used to be kind of dorky and shy, is now sixteen and gorgeous. Well, he kept talking about himself the whole time — like how many touchdowns he was scoring, which vitamins he took, the best kind of white socks to wear. *Boring!* And of course, Keisha acted as if he was just fascinating. Later we joked about him and Keisha seemed a little friendlier. But by that time we had to leave."

"You need some special TLC," Claudia said. She reached under her bed and pulled out another box. "How about a Ring Ding?"

Jessi laughed and took one. "Okay. They look better than those other things you were passing around."

"You know, going back to your old town can be weird," Stacey said. "Everything changes. The last time I went to New York, it didn't even feel like my neighborhood. My very favorite restaurant had become an ugly clothes boutique, and this old movie theater was being torn down to make an apartment building."

"Not to mention Laine," Claudia said.

"Right!" Stacey replied. "You can't even count on your old friends."

Laine had been Stacey's best friend in New York. But after Stacey moved to Stoneybrook, Laine changed. She became really snobby and cold.

Listening to Jessi and Stacey made my heart sink. What was going to happen to me? What about *my* friends and *my* neighborhood? At least Jessi and Stacey only went on short visits, so they could leave when the going got rough.

I had made a stupid mistake, I just knew it. I was going to be like ET, the extraterrestrial, when I returned to California. No one would know what to make of me. No one would want to be friends with a girl who planned to leave in six months!

Before long, *I* was the one looking gloomily out the window. Kristy had launched into this huge description of her Saturday at the Papadakises', and everybody else was laughing. In my mind I saw a split-screen image. On the left side, the BSC members (minus me) were building a snowman on a crisp wintry day, throwing snowballs and sipping thermoses of hot chocolate. On the right, I was sitting in traffic on the Santa Ana Freeway in California, listening to holiday music on the car radio and looking through smog at the red-and-green cellophane wreaths hanging on the street lights.

Whoa, Dawn, ease up! I told myself.

I tried to pay attention to the meeting. Kristy was now talking about Run for Your Money, which was only five days away.

"We're actually going to form two teams," she was saying. "Watson, me, Karen, Charlie, and Emily Michelle — and Mom, David Michael, Sam, Andrew, and Nannie. Unless Emily Michelle freaks out and has to be on Nannie's team."

"We're forming two teams, too!" Mal said, "but the triplets want to participate in, like, every single event."

"I'm trying to get my family interested in the pie-eating contest," Claudia said. "But Janine found out there's going to be a team trivia quiz event, so I will probably smile stupidly while Janine and my parents answer all the questions."

"We're going to enter Squirt in the baby race," Jessi piped up. "I want the rest of us to do the triathlon, which is a short race, a couple of low hurdles, and a long jump."

An idea hit me. I couldn't believe no one had thought of it yet. "Hey, what about us?" I said.

"Huh?" Claudia replied.

"A Baby-sitters Club team," I explained. "A person can be on more than one team, right? So each of us can be on a family team *and* a BSC team! We don't have to be in a lot of events, just one or two."

"Pretty good idea," Kristy admitted.

"Yeah!" a couple of the others said.

"Hey, there's a revised list of events in the *Stoneybrook News* today." Claudia grabbed a newspaper from the mess beside her bed. "Let's figure out what to enter."

We pored over the listing. People had been calling in with suggestions, so all kinds of new contests had been added. (One was "water balloon hot potato," thanks to the triplets, I'll bet.)

"Limbo dancing?" Claudia said.

"Uh, next suggestion," Stacey replied.

"Nerf home run derby?" Kristy read.

"You do that one alone," said Mary Anne.

"Pet races!" Mallory exclaimed.

"I don't think we qualify," Jessi said.

We finally narrowed it down to dance relay race (you pass a baton like in a relay race, but instead of running you dance), and and event called Mondo Ball (each team has to try to maneuver this gigantic ball from one side of the field to the other).

By the end of the meeting, I was feeling much better. I was even looking forward to my trip again.

I decided to call my dad that evening. He was just as happy and friendly as ever — and incredibly excited about my visit. Jeff was practically bursting with plans for us.

You know what? I didn't care about what might have changed in California. My real reason for going out there was to see Dad and Jeff.

And *they* hadn't changed a bit.

CHAPTER 10

Thursday

Today I sat for the
Pike kids with Mallory.
It was a pretty normal
day. We played in the
yard. Nothing much
else to say.

Now, do you believe a word of that?

Mary Anne is very smart, but she does *not* know how to lie. At least she could have written something a little more creative.

The truth was, she and Mal did a *lot* with the kids. But she didn't want to mention what, because it was a secret.

Mom drove her to the Pikes', which seemed a little weird to me, since they live just down the street. Mom insisted she had to go to the supermarket, and she was dropping Mary Anne off on the way.

Uh-huh.

Well, she went to the supermarket, all right — but *with* Mary Anne. To buy ingredients for my surprise farewell party, which was to be held on Sunday, the day after Run for Your Money!

(Luckily, I didn't find out about this until the party. I *love* surprises!)

The Pike kids spilled out of the house when Mary Anne and Mom arrived.

"I'll take in the bag with the chocolate chips!" Nicky yelled.

"What makes you think we bought chocolate chips?" Mary Anne asked.

"You didn't?" Adam said, wide-eyed.

"Dawn eats only health food," Mary Anne said. "So we're making a broccoli soufflé and preparing raw vegetables with dip."

The kids stared at her in shock. Mary Anne grinned and said, "Gotcha."

"Let me see!" Byron cried. He grabbed a grocery bag right out of her hand.

"Careful — " Mary Anne warned.

Rrrrrip! Out came chocolate chips, devils' food cake mix, potato chips, pretzels, and a frozen tofu-rhubarb pie.

Can you guess which one of those items was left on the sidewalk by the kids?

Anyway, Mary Anne and Mom brought the rest of the stuff in. Mrs. Pike ran downstairs, gave the sitters some last-minute instructions, and left with Mom.

The kitchen was instant chaos. Claire had pulled up a chair so she could help at the counter. Nicky was trying to pull it out from underneath her. Adam was bopping Vanessa on the head with a wire whisk. Margo had managed to open the flour sack and was making herself a white beard and mustache.

Phweeeeeeet!

Mary Anne jumped. The kids shut up.

Mallory was standing by the sink, a huge silver whistle in her mouth. Her face lit up. "Hey, this thing really works!"

"Where did you get that?" Adam asked.

"Dad bought it," Mal replied. "He thought we might need it for Run for Your Money."

"Let me try!" Jordan cried.

Mal should have tied the whistle around her neck. Before she could pull it away, Jordan grabbed it and started blowing.

"Me too!" six other voices called.

Mary Anne said she almost lost her hearing. Finally Mallory managed to grab the whistle away from Margo.

"Hey, what about me?" Claire complained.

"This was a mistake," Mal said.

"Waaaaaaahh!" Claire replied, falling to the floor.

"Baby!" Nicky taunted.

"I'm not a babyyyyyyy!" Claire cried.

"All right!" Mal held out the whistle. "One blow — and in the living room!"

Claire ran off and actually obeyed.

When she returned, preparations for a cake had already begun. (Actually, the tofu-rhubarb pie was for me. Most of the rest of the baking was for the invited guests — which included everyone in the BSC, their siblings, and a bunch of other sitting charges.)

"Can I crack the eggs? Can I?" Margo asked, grabbing an egg.

Splat.

It did crack. On the floor.

"Oops," Margo said sheepishly.

"That's okay," Mal said. "You know how to clean it up."

Sllllllosh! "Whoa!" Byron went sliding across the floor on the egg.

"Byronnn!" Mal moaned.

"Gross!" Adam yelled. "Let me try!"

"No!" said Mary Anne and Mal together.

As the first major cleanup of the day began, Vanessa danced around the room, composing a farewell poem aloud: "Dawn, Dawn, please don't go; we all love you so. . . ." When the floor was eggless, Mary Anne patiently helped Claire measure out sugar from a canister — while Adam kept licking his fingers and sticking them inside. Jordan and Byron played catch with the bag of chocolate chips, keeping it from Nicky.

And soon . . . there were visitors!

Stacey and Kristy had arrived with their charges. (Stace was sitting for Charlotte Johanssen and Kristy was sitting for the Barrett kids.) Mr. and Mrs. Pike had agreed to let them come over to help.

"I want to help with the cake!" Buddy Barrett insisted.

"I want to play!" shouted his sister Suzi.

"Oooh, you're making chocolate chip cookies?" Charlotte asked when she saw the game of catch.

"Give it to me!" Nicky screamed.

"Whoa . . . *whoa, listen up!*" Kristy put two

fingers in her mouth and whistled.

It made Mal's metal whistle sound dainty. All noise instantly stopped. (Leave it to Kristy.)

"Okay, we have to organize here," Kristy said. "We need a decorations committee, a baking committee, and a planning committee for games."

The kids all began shouting at once. In no time, the kitchen crew had shrunk to Margo, Nicky, Claire, and Buddy. Adam, Jordan, and Char agreed to plan the games; and Byron, Vanessa, and Suzi became the decoration team (with the "help" of little Marnie Barrett).

Of course, things didn't go perfectly. Byron almost fainted blowing up balloons. Marnie taped her fingers together and spilled Elmer's glue on the rug. Buddy dropped a head of garlic in the cake mix (unpeeled, thank goodness). The games committee argued over everything (Adam kept suggesting sports-type things, Jordan wanted only video games, and Charlotte insisted on quiet activities like dictionary and Twister). Vanessa disappeared into her bedroom and wasn't heard from for about an hour.

Finally around one o'clock everybody took a break. "All hands outside for playtime!" Kristy announced.

"Yeaaa!" the kids shouted. Everybody ran

out the back door (except for the food handlers, who had considerable washing up to do first).

Mary Anne ran upstairs to get Vanessa. She found her curled up on her bed, sniffling quietly, her eyes watery. A pad of paper and a pencil were lying next to her.

"What's wrong?" Mary Anne asked, sitting down.

"N-n-nothing," Vanessa said.

Out of the corner of her eye, Mary Anne glanced at the pad of paper. On it was a long farewell poem to me.

"Are you sad about Dawn leaving?" Mary Anne asked.

Vanessa nodded.

"Yeah, I'm going to miss her, too.

"She's your *sister*," Vanessa said sympathetically.

"I know. May I read it?"

"Uh-huh."

Well, you know Mary Anne. The waterworks began right away.

"Mary Anne, are you okay?" Vanessa asked.

Mary Anne wiped her eyes. "It's *beautiful*. Would you mind if I read it to the others?"

"You like it?"

"I love it."

Vanessa grinned. "Okay!"

They went out to the backyard. Somehow the four baby-sitters managed to gather the kids around the picnic table. Mallory was elected to read the poem (Mary Anne wasn't sure she'd make it through dry-eyed).

The poem went like this:

Dawn, Dawn, please don't go,
We all love you so.
Your nice to us, you make us smile
We love your hair, your laugh, your stile.
When you're away in California
We'll be so sad, we'll really mourn moarn ya.

"That doesn't rhyme," Adam volunteered.
"She's not *dying*," Jordan remarked.
"Shhhhh!" Kristy said.

Mallory continued:

We wish you luck, tho you upset us
Please, please, please, Dawn, don't forget us.

"Too many pleases," Adam murmured.

But his comment faded into the air. All the kids were looking sad. Mary Anne was dabbing her eyes.

Sigh. I have the best friends, don't I?

CHAPTER 11

"On your marks . . . get set . . . go!"

I was running, carrying a suitcase in each hand and a pack on my back.

My feet weren't even touching the ground. I passed Richard, Mom, and every member of the BSC except Mary Anne, who was ahead of me. But I couldn't see the finish line anywhere. When I pulled even with Mary Anne, she smiled at me. "Okay," she said. "You can stop now. . . . Dawn? *Dawn?*"

I couldn't stop. I was flying. Signs whizzed by me: *Ohio, Minnesota, Nebraska, Utah*. Finally I made out a huge sign that said WELCOME TO PALO CITY. Dad and Jeff were next to it, but they didn't see me. "Dad!" I screamed.

"Dawn?" Mary Anne said.

My eyes snapped open. "Huh?"

Mary Anne was leaning over my bed. "Are you okay? You were really tossing and turning."

"Yeah, just a dream," I mumbled.

"Well, hurry and come downstairs. We're having a power breakfast!" With a big smile, Mary Anne left.

I sat up and let the dream fade from my mind. Time for a reality check. I was in my room, and it was Saturday, the day of Run for Your Money. I glanced outside my window. Clouds were whipping by, but the weather didn't look too bad.

Suddenly I was in the real world. This was going to be a big day, and I was *psyched*.

I put on my one-piece bathing suit, then threw a sweat suit over it, and jammed my feet into a pair of sneakers. As I ran downstairs, the smell of pancakes and eggs and bacon hit me full-force.

I could do without the pig parts, but I *love* pancakes and I was even in the mood for eggs.

Mom was racing around the kitchen, dressed in very chic running shorts, with a matching top, leg warmers, and brand-new white sneakers. Richard was wearing a baggy, stiff pair of jeans; a paint-stained sweat shirt; and his brown, hideous "comfortable walking shoes." Mary Anne was busily pouring orange juice and setting the table.

"Power up!" Richard called out, flapping pancakes onto a plate.

"The breakfast of champions!" Mom said, making a muscle with her left arm. She was cutting green peppers into these huge, unusual shapes.

"Can I help?" I asked.

"Sure," Mom said. "I was making you a vegetarian omelet."

"Thanks," I said. "I'll take over if you want."

No protest from Mom. Now, I love her and she has many special talents. Unfortunately cooking is not one of them. I made sure to cut the peppers into sizes that wouldn't choke me, then went to work on the mushrooms.

Before long we were sitting down to the most humongous breakfast I've ever eaten. We chomped away like crazy, especially Richard. "I got up early for calisthenics and a jog," he boasted.

"Three pushups and halfway around the block," Mom said.

"Well, it's been awhile," Richard replied.

We scarfed down almost all the food and barreled outside. Mary Anne brought along a hat with a visor and three different bottles of sunblock (her skin is extremely sensitive to the sun). "Gentlemen, start your engine!" Richard called out as he turned the ignition.

"Dad, you are so goofy today," Mary Anne said.

"Gorsh!" Richard replied in a Goofy voice.

We sped to the high school, laughing all the way. Even before we arrived, we could feel the excitement. Three blocks away, cars were bumper-to-bumper, honking horns. Kids were leaning out of windows, cheering and waving banners. We ended up parking about a block away.

Well, you should have seen the high-school playing field. It was *jammed*. Things had been piled along the sidelines — potato sacks, boxes of bandannas for three-legged races, ropes for tug-of-war, hoses, balloons, buckets, balls, inflatable paddles. This huge blob (which I assumed was the Mondo Ball) was resting against the stands. Other stuff was still being piled on. On one side of the field were concession stands, and a couple of rides for kids (a Ferris wheel and rotating spaceships). The midway games — pinball and video machines, ring tosses, archery — were on the other side. Balloons and pennants waved everywhere — Lawrenceville's in the far stands, Stoneybrook's in the near ones.

Behind the south goalpost, the scoreboard looked like this:

Stoneybrook   Lawrenceville

"This is sooooo cool!" Mary Anne squealed.

"Nifty setup," Richard said.

We went straight to a sign-in booth. The woman there gave us a long timetable of events. She signed us up for tug-of-war, the baton relay, and the potato sack race.

"What about the underwear race?" I asked.

Mom gave Richard a Look. He cleared his throat and said, "Yes, well, I'm afraid I put the kibosh on that one."

"He refused to come unless we substituted something else," Mom explained.

"Maybe next year." Richard's face was turning red just talking about it.

"What's a kibosh?" I asked Mary Anne as we walked to the stands.

"A Dad word," she said. "It means to say no to something."

"Dawn! Mary Anne!" Kristy's voice shouted from the stands.

"Hi!" Mary Anne yelled back. My family

climbed the bleachers and took seats next to the Brewer/Thomases.

"I am psyched!" Kristy announced. "We're doing the Nerf home run derby, the three-legged race . . ."

I should probably explain Run for Your Money in more detail. It was divided into two parts. The first half consisted of more standard events, the second half of the weird ones (including the ones the BSC had entered). Many events ran at the same time, with referees for each one. Each team scored two points for a win, one for a tie, and none for a loss. The refs kept scorecards, and "runners" circulated the field, collecting the cards to bring to the master scorekeeper.

The Schafer/Spier events were in the first half, beginning with the tug-of-war. We played a family named the Medallises, from Lawrenceville. They also had two eighth-grade girls.

"Everybody here?" asked the referee, who was the owner of a music store at the local mall.

"Yes, sir," Mr. Medallis said, picking up one end of the rope. Then he looked at us with a smile. "You ready to be beaten silly?"

One of the girls rolled her eyes. *"Da-ad."*

"We'll see about that!" Richard answered. "Come on."

Oh, well, boys will be boys.

"Ready . . . set . . . go!" the ref said.

The Medallises were strong — but we were stronger. "Pullll," Mom grunted. *"Pullllll."*

We lurched backward. The Medallises fell to the ground in a heap.

"The winners — the Schafer/Spiers!" the ref called out. "Two points, Stoneybrook."

We hugged each other. We were two of the first points won that day! Then Mary Anne insisted we shake hands with the other family (what a good sport).

We celebrated our victory by getting some drinks at a concession stand. We said hi to the Newtons, the Barretts, and about a million other people. Then we watched Kristy's family win a three-legged contest, and the Kishis lose a relay race. Before long the scoreboard said Stoneybrook 24, Lawrenceville 8. Yea!

Next we ran the potato sack race. Our opponent was this incredibly enthusiastic family, the Smiths, who had a boy and a girl. As soon as we met them, one of the boys said, "You're *sisters*? You don't even look alike."

I don't know why that bothered me, but it did. Mary Anne cheerfully explained that we were a stepfamily, and the race began.

We lost that one. The baton relay was next, and we lost that, too. Mary Anne was very good-natured about it. She kept on saying,

"Between my dad and me, I'm glad we won *anything*."

But our mood had sunk a little, and Mom could tell.

"Hey, how about some pinball, Dawn?" she asked.

"Sure."

As we walked to the midway games, I looked around at the crowd. I wondered how many other people were part of stepfamilies. I saw a lot of look-alike siblings.

Everyone seemed somehow more . . . warm and excited than we did. I kept telling myself that was ridiculous, but it wasn't.

I knew why, too. They were real families. They knew they were going to live together, year in and year out. Not partial families, with one member going away for months at a time. I had one foot in Stoneybrook and the other in Palo City. No wonder we lost. I was pulling us apart.

I felt an awful twisty sensation in my stomach. How can you love two separate families and not feel like an outcast, or a traitor?

One thing was for sure. I needed a good game of pinball.

I took a peek at the scoreboard as Mom and I started to play. It looked like this:

Stoneybrook   Lawrenceville

Suddenly I couldn't wait for the BSC events to start.

CHAPTER 12

"And then Becca decided her sneakers were too tight, just as the referee yelled, 'Go!' " Jessi said.

It was halftime at Run for Your Money. The score was now Stoneybrook 97, Lawrenceville 94. All seven of us regular BSC members had decided to get together to find lunch at a concession stand. Everyone had a crazy story to tell about her family's events. Jessi's saga was about the triathlon.

"So Becca just *sat* there, screaming 'Do-over, do-over!' " Jessi went on. "But she wouldn't wear the sneakers, and Daddy wouldn't let her run in bare feet. Well, she sulked for about an *hour,* until we entered Squirt in the baby race. *He* wouldn't go in the right direction, because he kept wanting to hug Becca. He felt bad for her."

"That is so cute!" Stacey said.

"Remember the rolling race we practiced?"

Mal asked. "Well, Adam refused to do it with Jordan because he was too embarrassed to hold hands."

We groaned.

"I thought my family had done great in the three-legged race," Kristy said, "until Mom noticed that David Michael had used one of her silk scarves as a binding. Whoa, was she angry."

We walked from stand to stand, talking and laughing. Each time we stopped, everyone looked at Stacey and me to see if the food would be all right for our "diets."

Do you know what it's like to be a vegetarian surrounded by nothing but hot dogs, hamburgers, sausage, and fried chicken? Torture!

We finally settled on a stand that sold corn on the cob and bags of peanuts. I was still full from our power breakfast, so that was okay.

As we wandered over to the midway games, Mr. Kishi called out, "Hello, girls!" He and Mrs. Kishi were playing foosball against Janine. Honestly, I had never seen that girl move so fast. She was grabbing those knobs as if her life depended on it, shouting and laughing and having the best time.

We looked at Claudia. She smiled and shrugged. "The girl is crazed. I always knew there was an animal hiding inside her."

Just as we sat down in the stands, a voice boomed out, "Attention, please. Will everyone take your places for the second half of Run for Your Money!"

We checked our list. In five minutes we were scheduled for the dance relay race.

By one of the goalposts, an official was inserting a cassette into a huge tape deck with twin speakers. We met our Lawrenceville opponents, seven girls about our age.

The referee was this prim old woman, who said, "Stoneybrook is Lane One, and Lawrenceville is Lane Two. You'll see six orange marks ahead of you in each lane, one for each teammate in the relay. If anyone drops the baton, the team is disqualified. Now, we're going to play a pretty fast tune, so you can really *boogie down*."

We burst into giggles at that. Then we took our marks. Kristy was first in the relay, I was second, then Mary Anne, Stacey, Mal, Claudia, and Jessi.

When the ref said, "Go!" a rock dance tune started blaring. Kristy froze. Her face turned beet red.

The girl on the other team was gyrating down the track, her hair swinging back and forth. Her teammates were doubled over laughing.

Well, Kristy may have been embarrassed,

but she was also losing. And Kristy hates to lose.

She began bopping down the track, somehow moving her legs forward very fast. She looked . . . well, dorky would be an understatement. *We* were all cracking up.

I was next. Let me tell you, it is hard to run and dance at the same time — especially when you feel like a total fool. Crowds were forming on the sidelines, howling at us. I could see Jamie Newton staring in shock, as if something were wrong with us.

The teams were neck-and-neck to the last dancer. That's where we had our secret weapon — Jessi Ramsey, star ballerina.

You should have seen her. She did these incredible spinning leaps (*tour jetés*, she called them). The other girl stopped and gaped in amazement.

"The winner is Stoneybrook!" the referee called out.

"Yea, Jessi!" We crowded around her for a group hug. One of the Lawrenceville girls came over and started asking Jessi about her dance classes.

After they put our score up, the scoreboard read Stoneybrook 99, Lawrenceville 98.

Mondo Ball was a few events away. We watched the Papadakis team lose the basketball shooting contest. We half-expected Linny

109

to throw a tantrum, but instead Hannie started to cry — and Linny *comforted* her.

Some other highlights: The Barretts won a game of leap frog, but Buddy hit his head on a goalpost while dancing around in triumph. One of the Pike teams won at water balloon hot potato, after spraying the referee. The Arnolds lost the underwear race, mostly because they were laughing too hard; and Charlotte's dog, Carrot, escaped from a pet race to chase after a squirrel.

Stoneybrook was behind 113–112 when Mondo Ball was called. We ran out to the field and watched a team of four grownups roll this unbelievable *thing* toward us. It was more like a blimp than a ball.

"Are we sure we want to do this?" Claudia asked.

"Where's your team spirit?" Kristy replied.

"That thing's going to swallow us up!" Mal cried.

"Okay, teams, line up on either side of the Mondo Ball!" the referee called out.

It was now or never. We stood in the shadow of this six-foot-high globe.

"Ready . . . set . . . go!"

Well, you don't *know* what trying to move that thing was like. If you pushed it, your hands sunk in to it, so you had to throw your body against it. Then, if the people on the other side pushed harder than you, the ball would sort of glom over you.

Mondo Ball bounced and skidded and glommed up and down the field. It was impossible to get control of it. Half the time neither team even knew which direction we were going. At one point Stacey jumped on it and rolled all the way over the top.

Somehow we maneuvered the ball over to the Lawrenceville side. I think it was luck, but Kristy insists we did it on our own.

The referee blew a whistle. "Points to Stoneybrook!"

"Yeeeee-hah!" Kristy shouted.

We were thrilled. Two events, two victories. Mondo Ball instantly became a crowd favorite. (After us, teams were lining up to play for the rest of the afternoon.)

We stuck together till the end, cheering on our friends and playing midway games. Kristy even managed to hand out a couple of BSC fliers (can you believe it?). At one point, Logan showed up and hung out with us. (He'd had to work that day, at his part-time busboy job.)

The last event ended at five o'clock sharp. Then the announcer said: "Ladies and gentlemen, we are now awaiting the final tally. The runners are handing in the scorecards, and the official scorer is adding everything up. If you'll bear with us . . ."

The noise level dropped. You could hear leaves rustling in the breeze. We were all huddled together in front of the stands, BSC members and families. None of us could sit down.

Soon the numbers on the scoreboard started to flip. When they stopped, the board looked like this:

Stoneybrook	Lawrenceville
105	182

We *screamed*. Even Richard was pumping his arms and hooting.

"Thank you, all participants!" the announcer continued. "The real winner of the day is Stoneybrook's chosen organization, the Housing Council, which will receive two-thirds of today's profits!"

Another big cheer rose up, this time from both sides of the field.

Me? I felt *much* better than I had earlier. I hadn't had so much fun in ages.

We hung out for a few minutes, everyone laughing and talking about the events of the day. Eventually Kristy called out, "Hey, where are we going to celebrate?"

"The Rosebud Cafe," Logan suggested. (That's where he works.)

We asked our parents, and they all said fine. It would be a pretty long walk downtown, but that didn't matter. In our moods, we probably could have walked to Nova Scotia.

As we wound our way through the crowds to the sidewalk, Kristy spotted her math teacher. She gasped. "Oh, my gosh, I just realized I forgot to bring my math book home for the assignment this weekend."

"You can borrow mine," Mary Anne said. "I'll drop it off tomorrow."

Kristy sighed with relief. "It's amazing how something like Run for Your Money takes over your *life*!"

It *was* amazing. Kristy never forgets things.

A moment later Shannon Kilbourne came running toward us. "Great job on the Mondo Ball!" she called out.

"You saw us?" Stacey asked.

"Yeah, I got here just in time."

We invited Shannon to the Rosebud, and she got permission from her parents to come with us. Soon the nine of us began walking downtown.

"You should have seen the look on your face when you rolled over that ball, Stacey," Kristy said.

"You should have seen the look on *your* face

113

during the dance relay," Stace replied.

Kristy cringed. "That was sooo embarrassing."

"My dad said he got a picture of you," Claudia said.

"No!" Kristy's jaw dropped.

"I think I'll frame it and hang it in my room," Claud added, tapping her chin.

"You can give a print to Dawn so she can show her friends in California," Mal suggested.

"Not funny," Kristy hissed.

Everyone stopped talking, until Shannon asked, "So, are you all packed, Dawn?"

"No," I answered. "It's hard to pack for so long."

"I still can't believe you're going for six months," Logan said.

Mary Anne stood up for me. "She needs to, Logan. You don't know what it's like to have two families."

"I'd probably do the same thing if I were her," Jessi added.

"Are you guys going to be all right with just six regular members now?" Shannon asked.

"We'll figure something out," Claudia replied.

"Yeah, I'm not worried." Kristy flashed me a smile. "The most important thing is for Dawn to be happy."

Whoa. Was that Kristy Thomas I was hearing? Boy, had she changed.

"Thanks, Kristy," I said. I wanted to say how much that meant to me, but I could tell she understood.

Our waiter at the restaurant was a good friend of Logan's. He led us to the best table in the place — right by the window.

One of the nice things about the Rosebud is you can yack as loudly as you want. And we did. We must have discussed every single minute of the day.

Almost everyone ordered monster sundaes. I thought Stacey would go into a diabetic coma just looking at them. (She and I ordered sane food — Caesar salad and soup.)

Soon we could see the sun setting outside the window. The buildings across the street seemed to glow with a warm amber color.

It was a perfect end to the day. I couldn't imagine being more content.

And I began to think I was crazy for wanting to give up my life in Stoneybrook.

CHAPTER 13

Do you love *The Wizard of Oz*? I do. Sometimes I feel like Dorothy, wanting so badly to go home. Other times I feel like the Scarecrow or the Cowardly Lion.

Sunday morning was the first time I'd felt like the Tin Man.

I could barely move. It felt as if my joints had rusted. When I sat up, I thought I heard myself creak.

I guess I must have overdone it at Run for Your Money. Carefully I stood up and hobbled across the room. Clutching the banister, I made my way downstairs.

Mary Anne was already dressed and puttering around in the kitchen. "Hi!" she said. "You look as achy as I feel."

"Uuuhhhhh," I replied, sinking into a chair. Out of the corner of my eye, I saw the stove clock. "Did I really sleep till ten-thirty?"

"I just got up myself," Mary Anne said. "What do you want for breakfast?"

"I'll get it." I shuffled over to the cupboard and grabbed the nearest box of cereal. Mary Anne got the milk out of the fridge for me. "Where're Mom and Richard?" I asked.

"Doing errands," Mary Anne answered.

I yawned and plopped down at the table again. "I am doing *nothing* today. I don't even want to move."

Mary Anne laughed. "I know what you mean. Are you almost finished?"

"Eating?" I replied. "Mary *Anne*, I just started."

"Oh, okay. I'll do the dishes when you're done . . . so you can shower and get dressed."

"Uh-huh."

"You know, I haven't seen you wear those nice cream-colored drawstring waist pants you bought last month, and that ribbed cotton T-shirt with the buttons down the front. That would look nice."

"Mm-hm."

I wondered what on earth had gotten into my sister. There I was, slurping cereal, my eyes barely open, looking forward to a day on which I had planned absolutely nothing — and Mary Anne was already dressing me.

The moment I finished my breakfast, Mary

Anne took away my bowl and put it in the sink. "Uh, I was kind of looking forward to seconds," I said.

"Oh, sorry. Well, Dad'll be back any minute. I guess it would be nice for us to be . . . you know, dressed and ready."

"Ready? For what?"

"You know . . . for the day. That's all. I mean, he may need us to do things. The normal stuff."

I shrugged. "Yeah. I guess."

"I was just thinking, I really adore that outfit," Mary Anne reminded me.

"Okay, okay, I'll wear it."

I began the long, *long* climb upstairs. Each step was fresh torture. When I reached the top, I was exhausted. But even though my body was a mess, my mind was finally waking up.

Something was going on. I knew it. Mary Anne *never* acted the way she had acted at breakfast. Why did she want me to get ready so fast? How come she kept talking about that new outfit? And where were Mom and Richard, really?

I didn't need to be a genius to figure out she had planned a surprise. That was it. People were coming over, and Mary Anne didn't want me looking like the Swamp Thing.

In the warm water of the shower, my muscles started to feel a lot better. I ran into my room and put on the outfit Mary Anne wanted. I made sure my hair was dried and combed, and I even put on a little bit of makeup.

I could hear noises downstairs. I slowed down a little. If Mary Anne was directing people into hiding places, I didn't want to spoil things.

After a few minutes, I stood up and stretched. "Oh, I feel much better!" I said loudly. "I'm all ready, Mary Anne."

"Great," Mary Anne called up.

"Here I come!"

"Okay."

I walked slowly down the stairs. Mary Anne smiled and said, "You look fabulous!"

I walked nonchalantly into the dining room. No one was there. I wandered into the living room, the den. Empty. No one behind couches or under tables.

Mary Anne was tidying up the house, not saying a word.

Ding-dong.

The doorbell! They were waiting outside, ready to come in. "Should I get it?" I asked.

"If you want," Mary Anne replied.

With my biggest smile, I flung the door open.

It was Richard. Alone. " 'Morning," he said. "I'm back."

I looked over his shoulder. I expected to see heads popping up from behind bushes.

Wrong.

"Any volunteers to accompany me on a dangerous mission to the grocery store?" Richard asked.

Mary Anne came into the living room. "Great," she said. "We weren't doing anything."

We walked out to the car. I began to feel excited again. Of course! They were *taking* me to a party.

Minutes later, Richard pulled up to our destination.

The grocery store.

We bought some detergent and paper towels and tuna. Then we left.

I sank into the backseat of my car. In my drawstring pants, I was sure I had looked smashing in the household goods aisle. Ho-hum.

"Didn't you want to drop off something at Kristy's?" Richard asked Mary Anne.

"Oh! Right, the math book she forgot!" Mary Anne said. She reached into the glove compartment. "I put it in here yesterday, just so I wouldn't forget — and then I forgot."

Richard drove across town. He pulled into the driveway of the Brewer mansion. "Try not to gab too much," Richard said. "Sharon'll be home soon."

"I'll stay in the car," I said.

"No, come on," Mary Anne insisted. "Kristy will want to see you."

Blink. The light went on in my mind. *This* was the party. They were waiting behind Kristy's front door. The math book was just a trick.

Mary Anne rang the bell, and Kristy answered right away. "Hi!" she said. "Hey, thanks for the book. I can't believe I forgot it."

The house was empty behind her, and quiet. No decorations, no nothing.

But it was okay. I could deal with it. I was a big girl.

"Oh!" Kristy suddenly said. "You will not believe the size of the zucchini Watson found in the vegetable garden! Want to take a look?"

"Sure," Mary Anne and I replied. See? All was not lost. Maybe I wasn't getting a party, but at least I'd get to see a very large vegetable.

Kristy led us through the huge house and out the back door. I walked through it, stifling a yawn.

"SURPRIIIIIISE!"

The yawn caught in my throat. My mouth froze in the open position.

A flash went off, blinding me. Great. Someone had taken a photo of me, looking like Monstro the Whale.

When my eyes cleared, I could see a crowd of smiling faces. Stacey, Claudia, Jessi, Mal, Logan, and Shannon were there, as well as a whole bunch of our charges: the Pike, Barrett, Newton, and Papadakis kids, and Charlotte Johanssen.

"Like the decorations?" Suzi Barrett asked. "I was on the committee."

"They're *beautiful!*" I said.

They were, too. A banner that said BON VOYAGE, DAWN! hung from Kristy's huge maple tree. Two picnic tables were set up with homemade California-theme centerpieces made of odds and ends and Elmer's glue: one was an airplane and the other was a round face with sunglasses. On the back wall of the house, the kids had put up a mural. The scene was a beach, with a blonde girl lazing in the sun and writing letters. On the sand next to her were envelopes, and on each one was written the name of one of my charges. Across the top was written WE LOVE YOU, DAWN! PLEASE WRITE!

"That's your going-away gift," Charlotte said to me. "We know just how to fold it so you can take it with you."

I looked at Mary Anne. For the first time in our lives I started crying first.

Then Vanessa decided to read her poem. Well, let me tell you, all us BSCers were basket cases. Kristy's lawn didn't need any watering after that. I started hugging everyone left and right. The kids stared at us blankly.

"Okay, enough mushy stuff," Jordan Pike said. "Time for blindman's buff!"

Guess who was the blind man? Yours truly. The games committee had really done its work. We played Pin the Tail on the Donkey, scatch, Red Light Green Light, and Twister. Some of the kids disappeared inside for video games, but Watson chased them back out.

All the while, Buddy kept asking Kristy, "Is it time for the cake yet?"

Finally Kristy could take it no longer. She, Buddy, Margo, Nicky, and Claire went into the kitchen. First Claire came out with a huge tray full of chocolate chip cookies. Then Buddy proudly displayed the cake, which was roughly the shape of a haystack and the color of mud. Its icing had been applied in thick globs.

"Yummmm!" the kids squealed.

Margo then appeared with bags of chips and pretzels, and Kristy brought out a punch bowl. Last came Nicky, who beamed as he held up the tofu-rhubarb pie. "Kristy said you'd like this best of all!" he announced.

"Oh, I will!" I replied. "I can't wait to eat it!"

As the kids crowded onto the benches, I began pouring drinks.

"Uh-uh-uh!" Logan said, waving me away. "You're the guest of honor."

I sat down with my tofu-rhubarb pie. A piece of chocolate icing flew by me from left to right. Buddy spat out a flake of garlic skin they hadn't seen in the cake. Claire got up from the table, clutching my leg for balance and leaving a large brown stain on my drawstring pants. I heard the trickle of apple juice seeping through the crack of the picnic table onto the deck floor. At the end of the table, Adam Pike began a burping contest that grew into an all-out war.

But you know what? It could have started snowing and I wouldn't have minded. I was on Cloud Nine.

It was a weekend I would never, ever forget.

CHAPTER 14

Monday. T minus five and counting. One more week of school, and then 'bye-'bye Stoneybrook.

Was I delirious? Was I tingling with excitement?

No. I was sitting up in bed, shaking off a night's sleep, and thinking.

Thinking about the terrific party the day before. Thinking about the great time I'd had at Run for Your Money and the Rosebud Cafe.

In five days I'd be thousands of miles from all of this.

Why?

The question kept repeating itself in my mind.

In a way, I wished I'd been having a horrible life in Stoneybrook. Maybe if my friends were mean, or if my home life was dull or if Mary Anne and I hated each other, maybe then leaving would be easy. I wouldn't be having second thoughts.

I stood up. I pulled some clothes from my drawers and closet. The smell of coffee wafted up from the kitchen. I could hear a newspaper rustling and my mom laughing at something Richard was saying.

Mom was acting so positive about my decision. I tried putting myself in her shoes. I would never forget the look on her face when I announced what I wanted to do. It was as if she'd aged ten years.

But since then she had really pulled herself together. So had Mary Anne and Kristy and all my other friends. Now they were supporting me, telling me how much I needed to go.

I guess they had no choice. They knew I was going, so they had to make the best of it. Better that than sit around feeling angry or sad. In a way, they were adjusting, that's all. Adjusting to what life would be like minus Dawn.

And they were doing a good job. *Too* good, I thought.

Okay, I hate to admit it, but it was kind of *flattering* to know how everyone really felt. It showed how much they cared. You know what I was thinking then? Everyone had adjusted so well, that if I'd suddenly decided *not* to go, they'd be disappointed!

Nah. Ridiculous. I tried to push those feelings out of my mind. I told myself to be thankful that I was leaving one happy life and going to another. Having two families made me twice as lucky as most kids, right?

Right. I looked in my mirror and smiled away my grouchy face.

But on the way downstairs, I had to work to keep that smile going.

"Good morning," everyone said.

No one talked about my trip, and I didn't bring it up. Mary Anne left a little early for school, because she was meeting Logan first. So I wolfed down breakfast and left the house alone. I was looking forward to school, to be honest. I figured it would take my mind off my dilemma.

I was wrong. A fog had settled over Stoneybrook that morning, and I think some of it got locked in my brain. I simply could *not* concentrate. What happened in homeroom? I don't even remember going. Math? English? Social studies? Beats me. At this rate, the teachers in Palo City were going to pack me up and send me back to Mrs. Amer with *defective* stamped across my forehead.

All kinds of doubts kept flooding in, stuff I'd never thought of before. Like *Dad's* point of view. I mean, think of it. My decision

127

couldn't have been easy for him, either. Setting up life as a single person, then having Jeff return unexpectedly to his life. Having to adjust to single parenthood. Working out a happy, stable life for Jeff. At least Mom had met someone else and remarried. Dad hadn't.

Well, he hadn't *married*, that is. But he *had* been dating. And he seemed pretty serious about Carol.

That was another thing. What about Dad's social life? How was he going to feel with *two* kids around the house?

I began thinking my trip might be terribly wrong.

You can imagine my relief when school ended. I was looking forward to the BSC meeting. I knew we'd talk about the weekend, and that would be fun.

Mary Anne and I arrived early, just in time to see Shannon and Jessi practicing a tap-dancing move. (Actually, on Claudia's carpet it was more like *thud*-dancing.)

"You really have to step *into* the floor," Shannon was staying. (She takes on-again, off-again tap classes.) "You're kind of floating. Now come on, *stamp*, step, falap, ball-change!"

"That is so hard on your shins," Jessi said. "It's not at all like ballet."

"Let me try!" Kristy stood up and began

stomping around as if she were trying to kill a cockroach. Shannon and Jessi cracked up. Then Claudia and Stacey decided to try. The walls began to shake.

"What's going on up there?" Janine finally called from her room. "Marching band practice?"

We burst into giggles. "Sorry!" Claudia yelled.

For the first time that day, my mind-fog was clearing. We settled into our regular positions — Kristy sitting on the director's chair; Claudia, Mary Anne, and I on the bed; Stacey on the desk chair; and Mal, Jessi, and Shannon on the floor. It was a ritual. We all did it automatically.

I was already feeling nostalgic about it. Claudia and Mary Anne would soon have a lot more room on the bed. I wondered how they felt about it. And was Shannon going to take my place? I hadn't expected her to be at the meeting. Had she changed her mind and decided to become the alternate officer?

"How's your honor society project going?" I asked her.

"Great, so far," she said. "It turns out we may not be meeting on Mondays, though, so maybe I can make those BSC meetings during the next two months." She shrugged. "At any rate, I'll help as much as I can."

"That's great," Mary Anne piped up. "And Logan told me today he'd try really hard to make himself available."

Kristy nodded. "Cool. I knew things would work out. I mean, this isn't perfect, but we'll do the best we can." Her eyes darted to the clock, just as it turned to 5:30. "This meeting shall come to order!"

"*Shall?*" Claudia said.

"Yeah, it sounds more official," Kristy replied.

"How about using, like, cometh," Claudia suggested. "This meeting shall cometh to order."

"Then you have to say 'Hear ye, hear ye!' " Stacey added.

"Heareth ye, heareth ye! Ye Olde Meeting of the Baby-sitters Club shall cometh to order!" Shannon announced.

Kristy giggled. "You guys are dweebs."

I wanted to laugh. Everybody else was laughing. So I tried, but it came out sounding fake.

Why? Well, when my fog finally disappeared, something happened. All my thoughts from the day swirled together, and I could see them clearly.

When my parents had been together, I once had to make a decision. It seemed important at the time, but now I don't remember exactly what it was — whether to join a club or something. Well, Dad gave me a great suggestion. He told me to draw a line down the middle of a piece of paper and label the columns PRO and CON. I'd list reasons *to* do whatever it was in the left column, reasons *not* to do it in the right. I would make my choice based on whichever list had the most items.

I was doing that in my head now. On the PRO side, for going to California, I listed these things:

1. Being with Dad and Jeff.
2. Seeing my old friends.
3. Being in California.

On the CON side:

1. Missing Mom.
2. Missing Mary Anne.
3. Missing the Baby-sitters Club.
4. Coming back to find the BSC didn't really need me after all.
5. Doing terribly in my new school.
6. Doing terribly when I come back to SMS.
7. Not getting along with Carol.
8. Putting too much pressure on Dad.
9. Having the kind of experience Jessi had in Oakley.

The list went on and on. But I didn't complete it. I didn't have to. A decision had planted itself in my brain. I couldn't believe I hadn't come to it earlier.

I had to announce it right away. Claudia and Mary Anne were in the middle of scheduling a sitting job for the next week, and they were having a hard time.

"Um, guys?" I said. "Don't worry about not scheduling me. Go ahead if you need to."

Claudia shook her head. "It's for a week from Thursday. You won't be here — unless you want to fly back to sit for the Prezziosos."

"I won't need to," I said. "I'm not going."

Claudia dropped the receiver. She quickly picked it up and said into it: "Uh, can I call you back? . . . Thanks, 'bye." *Click.* She hung up and stared at me. *"Whaaaaat?"*

"I'm staying here. I've changed my mind."

The room was so quiet I could swear I heard the sun setting. I began laughing. "Well . . . say something!"

"Are you sure?" Mary Anne asked.

"Mm-hm."

"Who-o-oa," Kristy said under her breath. A smile began flickering across her face.

Claudia let out a whooshing breath. "Okay, who's going to organize the Welcome Back party?"

Well, the meeting turned to chaos. Claudia went rummaging around for all the junk food she could find. Mary Anne grabbed a box of tissues and began wiping tears away. My friends asked me questions, but not many. I think they were afraid that if I thought about my decision too much, I might change my mind.

But the lists had made it clear. The score was at least twelve cons to three pros. I was staying.

At the end of the meeting, Mary Anne and I raced to our bikes. As we rode home, I thought and thought about my one remaining problem.

Breaking the news to my parents.

CHAPTER 15

A tear fell onto my book. There was only one word on the page, at the top: *JOURNAL*. I had written it in bold letters, with a felt-tip pen. I'd never kept a journal before, so I wanted to make a definite, strong statement. Now the ink on the letter *L* was all smudged, and the page was starting to pucker.

Oh, well. I guess a journal's supposed to be about feelings, and I'll always know what the tear was about.

I tried looking out the window, but the setting sun was too strong. Instead I sat back. My stomach was growling and tumbling, and suddenly I wished I hadn't eaten that huge plate of ravioli for dinner.

I was going to be getting another dinner soon, anyway.

Bing. A bell chimed, followed by a soft voice. "Good evening, folks. I'm Captain Jordan, and on behalf of the entire flight crew, I'd like to welcome you to transcontinental flight six-six-two to Los Angeles. We've been cleared for takeoff, so we're about to taxi onto the runway. The skies are looking pretty clear . . ."

This was it. I shielded my eyes and looked out the window again. This time I could make out the silhouettes of Mom, Richard, and Mary Anne against a window in the airport, staring at the plane. I waved, but they didn't see me.

Now my tears were dripping onto the handrest. Someone stirred in the seat next to me, but I didn't turn my head. I wanted to be alone with my thoughts. I had just spent the longest, toughest week of my life.

Okay. Let me start from the beginning. I guess that means Monday, after the BSC meeting.

I was sure I'd come to my final decision. Mary Anne and I got home in record time. I called an emergency family meeting during dinner, and Mary Anne sat next to me at the table.

Patiently I described my pro-and-con list to Mom and Richard. I apologized for messing up their plans and waffling back and forth, but my mind was made up. I wasn't going to California.

Mom nodded and smiled. The first thing she

said was, "Sweetheart, sometimes a decision like this can't be made by counting things on a list."

"But it was so lopsided," I said.

"I know," she replied. "But not each item is equally important."

Richard nodded. "Besides, you listed the pros and cons of moving to California. But you didn't list the pros and cons of staying in Stoneybrook."

Well, I exploded at that. "It sounds like you *want* me to go!"

"Oh, no! No, sweetheart, that's not it at all," Mom said. She sighed deeply, and her eyes began to water. "The list was a great idea. It shows how deeply you've been thinking about this. But I know you, Dawn. I know when you're speaking from your heart and when you're speaking from your brain."

She didn't need to say anymore. My anger started to melt into a little pool and trickle away. Mom was right. My poor little heart had been working overtime for weeks. The list had been a way to give it a rest and let my brain do the work.

Only Mom could see that. It must have been so hard for her to have to convince me to go. But she knew if I let the list make my decision, I'd regret it. "I guess we eventually might have the same problem again, huh?" I said.

Mom shrugged and looked downward sadly, and I thought about how much I loved her.

Next to me, Mary Anne was soaking a tissue. Even Richard had teary eyes. All week long I'd been wondering whether everyone really cared about me. I wasn't wondering anymore.

Our meeting lasted way past dinnertime. I began to talk once again about the reasons I was aching to go to California. That's what it was, an ache. And I realized it would have been impossible to cover it up.

That night I called my friends, one by one. They sounded sad, but I think they were kind of expecting my news. They'd scheduled me for one job the next week, but Kristy assured me she could cover it.

The rest of the week I packed and said lots of good-byes. I went shopping with Claudia and Stacey for new clothes. I had second (third? fourth?) thoughts, but not once did I change my mind again. Then on Friday I had a meeting with Mrs. Amer, who made me feel confident I'd do all right in my new school.

I took a mental picture of SMS as I left it on Friday afternoon, but I didn't say good-bye. *It'll be here in six months*, I thought, *barring an earthquake*. Thinking that made me laugh. I really am such a Californian.

At our Friday meeting BSC might as well have stood for the Bawlers and Snifflers Club. We could barely answer the phone. Claudia must have told four different parents she had a cold.

On our final bike ride home, I thought Mary Anne and I would both topple over. It's hard to see the street when your eyes are wet.

Between last-minute packing and shopping, Friday night and Saturday blazed by. Late in the afternoon, the doorbell rang. I ran to open it, with Mary Anne behind me.

Jessi, Mal, Kristy, Stacey, and Claudia were standing on the porch. They were dressed beautifully, holding out a wrapped present.

"Ohhhh, you *didn't*," I said. (Honestly, I don't how a person's body can keep producing so many tears. I thought mine would have been used up by then, but *noooooo*.)

"We did," Claudia said.

"Should I open it?" I asked.

"Yes," Mal said. "You'll need it on the plane."

I ripped open the wrapping and the box. Inside was a gorgeous, leather-bound book of blank pages.

I gasped. "I *love* it!" I said.

"It's a journal," Mallory explained. "So you can write down everything that happens."

"And then show us," Stacey added.

"We figured you might get rusty while you were away from the BSC notebook," Kristy said.

"Oh, thanks! I will miss you guys — so — " I couldn't finish. I just threw my arms open and everyone fell into them. We must have stood there for twenty minutes, crying and hugging and I'll-miss-youing.

When they left, I felt a huge tug in my stomach. But I had to think of the flight then.

Mom, Richard, Mary Anne, and I loaded into the car around four o'clock and drove to the Rosebud Cafe for dinner. Logan was working, which was wonderful. I would have felt silly crying in front of a strange busboy.

Dinner was fun, but I think we were all a little nervous about getting stuck in a traffic jam on the way to the airport. I gulped down my ravioli (which, of course, I later regretted).

We reached the airport with plenty of time to spare, which turned out to be a bad idea. Mary Anne and I blubbered uncontrollably. Then Mom and I held onto each other as if we were permanently stuck.

You know what she whispered in my ear? Not "Write," or "Brush your teeth," or "Get good grades," or anything like that.

She said, "Let Daddy love you as much as I do."

I had to get on the plane fast before I dissolved into one huge tear.

The entire week flashed through my mind in the time it took the captain to finish his speech. As the "Fasten Your Seatbelt" sign came on, I looked out the window again.

Mom and Richard and Mary Anne were not there anymore. I turned to my book and began writing:

JOURNAL

Saturday

It's 6:45. The sun is setting behind the airport terminal. In five hours, it will be 8:45, and I will be home . . . .

I was a little surprised I'd written the word *home*. I crossed it out and wrote *in California*.

But neither one seemed exactly right. I stopped writing and stared at the words for a long time.

Then I made a decision. I'd leave it. After all, it didn't really matter. I could always go back and change it if I wanted.

Six months was a long time.

About the Author

ANN M. MARTIN did *a lot* of baby-sitting when she was growing up in Princeton, New Jersey. Now her favorite baby-sitting charge is her cat, Mouse, who lives with her in her Manhattan apartment.

Ann Martin's Apple Paperbacks include *Yours Turly, Shirley; Ten Kids, No Pets; With You and Without You; Bummer Summer;* and all the other books in the Baby-sitters Club series.

She is a former editor of books for children, and was graduated from Smith College. She likes ice cream, the beach, and *I Love Lucy;* and she hates to cook.

Look for BSC #68

JESSI AND THE BAD BABY-SITTER

"Where have you been?" Kristy demanded.

A look of bewilderment came over Wendy's face. I could see she didn't understand why Kristy had spoken so sharply. "I had a baby-sitting job, but the mother was late coming home," she explained. "Did any jobs come in for me?"

"There would have been if you'd been here," Kristy told her. I'm sure Wendy could see she was pretty angry. But, she didn't react the way I would have. I'd have been mortified and apologetic. Wendy wasn't, though. She grew angry in return.

"What's the big deal?" she asked. "Can't Mary Anne tell from that record book thing whether or not I'm free? Why do I have to be here."

"Because you have to be," Kristy said, her

face turning pink as she held back her anger.

"We're all expected to come to every meeting unless it's a real emergency," I explained.

"Well, this was an emergency," Wendy insisted. "I couldn't leave the kids by themselves."

"Next time call," Mary Anne sid. "And why did you take a job without telling us?"

"What do you mean?" asked Wendy.

"That's the second club rule you've broken," Kristy jumped in.

"I don't know what you're talking about!" Wendy said irritably. Her hands were on her hips and I could tell she wasn't liking the treatment she was receiving from Kristy.

"First, you were late without calling, then you took a job that wasn't offered to the rest of the club," Kristy spoke cooly.

"And you saying I have to hand my regular jobs over to the club?!" Wendy cried indignantly.

"We all share jobs," said Stacey. "Even if a client asks for one certain sitter, we say that we can't do that. That's the only way it will be fair."

"Okay, I can see that, I guess," Wendy conceded reluctantly. 'Sorry. And next time I'll call."

**Read all the books
in the Baby-sitters Club series
by Ann M. Martin**

#40 *Claudia and the Middle School Mystery*
Can the Baby-sitters find out who the cheater is at SMS?

#41 *Mary Anne vs. Logan*
Mary Anne thought she and Logan would be together forever . . .

#42 *Jessi and the Dance School Phantom*
Someone — or some*thing* — wants Jessi out of the show.

#43 *Stacey's Emergency*
The Baby-sitters are so worried. Something's wrong with Stacey.

#44 *Dawn and the Big Sleepover*
One hundred kids, thirty pizzas — it's Dawn's biggest baby-sitting job ever!

#45 *Kristy and the Baby Parade*
Will the Baby-sitters' float take first prize in the Stoneybrook Baby Parade?

#46 *Mary Anne Misses Logan*
But does Logan miss *her*?

#47 *Mallory on Strike*
Mallory needs a break from baby-sitting — even if it means quitting the club.

#48 *Jessi's Wish*
Jessi makes a very special wish for a little girl with cancer.

146

THE BABY-SITTERS CLUB®

by Ann M. Martin

More titles... ➤

❑ MG44970-2	#49 Claudia and the Genius of Elm Street	$3.25
❑ MG44969-9	#50 Dawn's Big Date	$3.25
❑ MG44968-0	#51 Stacey's Ex-Best Friend	$3.25
❑ MG44966-4	#52 Mary Anne + 2 Many Babies	$3.25
❑ MG44967-2	#53 Kristy for President	$3.25
❑ MG44965-6	#54 Mallory and the Dream Horse	$3.25
❑ MG44964-8	#55 Jessi's Gold Medal	$3.25
❑ MG45657-1	#56 Keep Out, Claudia!	$3.25
❑ MG45658-X	#57 Dawn Saves the Planet	$3.25
❑ MG45659-8	#58 Stacey's Choice	$3.25
❑ MG45660-1	#59 Mallory Hates Boys (and Gym)	$3.25
❑ MG45662-8	#60 Mary Anne's Makeover	$3.50
❑ MG45663-6	#61 Jessi's and the Awful Secret	$3.50
❑ MG45664-4	#62 Kristy and the Worst Kid Ever	$3.50
❑ MG45665-2	#63 Claudia's Friend Friend	$3.50
❑ MG45666-0	#64 Dawn's Family Feud	$3.50
❑ MG45667-9	#65 Stacey's Big Crush	$3.50
❑ MG45575-3	Logan's Story Special Edition Readers' Request	$3.25
❑ MG44240-6	Baby-sitters on Board! Super Special #1	$3.95
❑ MG44239-2	Baby-sitters' Summer Vacation Super Special #2	$3.95
❑ MG43973-1	Baby-sitters' Winter Vacation Super Special #3	$3.95
❑ MG42493-9	Baby-sitters' Island Adventure Super Special #4	$3.95
❑ MG43575-2	California Girls! Super Special #5	$3.95
❑ MG43576-0	New York, New York! Super Special #6	$3.95
❑ MG44963-X	Snowbound Super Special #7	$3.95
❑ MG44962-X	Baby-sitters at Shadow Lake Super Special #8	$3.95
❑ MG45661-X	Starring the Baby-sitters Club Super Special #9	$3.95

Available wherever you buy books...or use this order form.

Scholastic Inc., P.O. Box 7502, 2931 E. McCarty Street, Jefferson City, MO 65102

Please send me the books I have checked above. I am enclosing $ —————
(please add $2.00 to cover shipping and handling). Send check or money order - no
cash or C.O.D.s please.

Name ——————————————————————————————————

Address ————————————————————————————————

City———————————————— State/Zip ————————————

Please allow four to six weeks for delivery. Offer good in the U.S. only. Sorry, mail orders are not
available to residents of Canada. Prices subject to change.

Don't miss out on The All New

Fan Club

Join now!
Your one-year membership package includes:

- The exclusive Fan Club T-Shirt!
- A Baby-sitters Club poster!
- A Baby-sitters Club note pad and pencil!
- An official membership card!
- The exclusive *Guide to Stoneybrook!*

Plus four additional newsletters per year

so you can be the first to know the hot news about the series — Super Specials, Mysteries, Videos, and more — the baby-sitters, Ann Martin, and lots of baby-sitting fun from the Baby-sitters Club Headquarters!

ALL THIS FOR JUST $6.95 plus $1.00 postage and handling! **You can't get all this great stuff anywhere else except THE BABY-SITTERS FAN CLUB!**

Just fill in the coupon below and mail with payment to: THE BABY-SITTERS FAN CLUB, Scholastic Inc., P.O. Box 7500, 2931 E. McCarty Street, Jefferson City, MO 65102.

THE BABY-SITTERS FAN CLUB

___ YES! Enroll me in The Baby-sitters Fan Club! I've enclosed my check or money order (no cash please) for $7.95

Name _____ Birthdate _____

Street _____

City _____ State/Zip _____

Where did you buy this book?

❏ Bookstore ❏ Drugstore ❏ Supermarket
❏ Book Fair ❏ Book Club ❏ other_____

BSFC593

How would YOU like to visit Universal Studios in Orlando, Florida?

Check out the sights!

Experience the rides!

Tour the Studios!

Enter THE BABY-SITTERS CLUB®

Summer Super Special Giveaway for your chance to win!

We'll send one grand prize winner and a parent or guardian on an all expense paid trip to Universal Studios in Orlando, Florida for 3 days and 2 nights!

25 second prize winners receive a Baby-sitters Club Fun Pack filled with a Baby-sitters Club T-Shirt, "Songs For My Best Friends" cassette, Baby-sitters Club stationery and more!

All you have to do is fill out the coupon below or write the information on a 3" x 5" piece of paper and mail to:

THE BABY-SITTERS CLUB SUMMER SUPER SPECIAL GIVEAWAY P.O. Box 7500, Jefferson City, MO 65102. Return by November 30 1993.

- -

THE SUMMER SUPER SPECIAL GIVEAWAY

Name _____ Birthdate _____

Address _____

City_____ State/Zip _____

Rules: Entries must be postmarked by November 30, 1993. Winners will be picked at random and notified by mail. No purchase necessary. Valid only in the U.S. Void where prohibited. Taxes on prizes are the responsibility of the winners and their immediate families. Employees of Scholastic Inc; its agencies, affiliates, subsidiaries, and their immediate families not eligible. For a complete list of winners, send a self-addresses stamped envelope to:The Baby-sitters Club Summer Super Special Giveaway, Winners List, after November 30 at the address provided above.

BSC693

THE BABY·SITTERS Club®

SPECIAL DELIVERY... FOR YOU!

The Baby-sitters have split up for vacation, but Kristy's in the hospital. How will the girls stay in touch?—A chain letter! Now *you* can open authentically stamped envelopes, unfold and read real letters in the baby-sitters' own hand—writing, and learn a special secret about each one of them — all in one spectacular, must—have book!

Real letters, cards, and even a friendship bracelet from the Baby-sitters Club!

The Baby-Sitters Club Chain Letter
by Ann M. Martin

Coming in September!

BSCL293

Create Your Own
Mystery Stories!

MYSTERY GAME !

WHO:	Boyfriend	**WHY:**	Romance
WHAT:	Phone Call	**WHERE:**	Dance

Use the special Mystery Case card to pick WHO did it, WHAT was involved, WHY it happened and WHERE it happened. Then dial secret words on your Mystery Wheels to add to the story! Travel around the special Stoneybrook map gameboard to uncover your friends' secret word clues! Finish four baby-sitting jobs and find out all the words to win. Then have everyone join in to tell the story!

**YOU'LL FIND THIS
GREAT MILTON BRADLEY GAME
AT TOY STORES AND BOOKSTORES
NEAR YOU!**

NOW PLAYING!

Home Video Collection

*Look for these
all new episodes!*

■

**Claudia and the Mystery
of the Secret Passage**

Dawn Saves the Trees

The Baby-sitters and the Boy Sitters

**Jessi and the Mystery
of the Stolen Secrets**

Stacey Takes a Stand

The Baby-sitters Remember

■

*Available wherever fun
videos are sold*

Distributed by

Kid Vision